Final Cover-Up

The Bones of Old Town

DAN PEDERSEN

FINAL COVER-UP

DAN PEDERSEN

Final Cover-Up

The Bones of Old Town

DAN PEDERSEN

FINAL COVER-UP

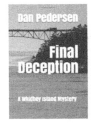   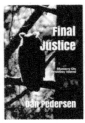 

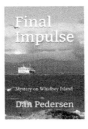  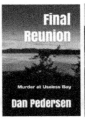  

In the order of publication.

Mysteries by the Author
Available from Whidbey Island bookstores and Amazon.com

Final Deception: *A Whidbey Island Mystery (book 1)*
Final Passage: *Mystery on the Alaska Ferry (book 2)*
Final Escape: *Mystery in the Idaho Sawtooths (book 3)*
Final Justice: *Mystery on Whidbey Island (book 4)*
Final Pursuit: *Mystery in the Adirondacks (book 5)*
Final Impulse: *Mystery on Whidbey Island (book 6)*
Final Descent: *Mystery on Whidbey Island (book 7)*
Final Reunion: *Murder at Useless Bay (book 8)*
Final Remains: *Mystery at Ebey's Landing (book 9)*
Final Cover-Up: *The Bones of Old Town (book 10)*

Cover: Oak Harbor Bay, by Dan Pedersen
Email inquiries to Dan Pedersen: *dogwood@whidbey.com*
Copyright © 2021 Dan Pedersen
All rights reserved. ISBN - 9798705159390

To My Silent Partner

This book introduces a new character, *Duncan*, my best friend and companion for more than a decade, until his death in 2020. He lived every day with the joy of new discoveries and filled my days with them, too.

Like the fictional *Duncan* in this book, the real *Duncan* came to us fearful and insecure after a shadowy past and a brush with death in a shelter that euthanizes unadopted dogs. My wife, Sue, and I worked with a canine behaviorist and watched *Duncan* become a calm, confident, wise and respectful friend – a testament to the power of kindness and consistency. He was never entirely "trained" and we didn't mind – we admired his spirit. He was a thinker, an *independent* thinker, not the worst quality in an investigator.

This is my tenth mystery in ten years, and *Duncan* was my silent partner for all those hours of writing. We walked miles together, exploring the places where ideas are born.

FINAL COVER-UP

Principal Characters
Grouped with related characters

Katarina (Kat) Brown – sheriff's deputy, Whidbey Island
Duncan – Kat's dog, a "Border Corgi"
Shane Lindstrom – sheriff's detective and Kat's mentor
Don Mosier – archaeologist, City of Oak Harbor
Roger Gray – retired sheriff's deputy, salmon fisherman
Dr. Ralph Emerson – county coroner

Elliott Langston – also known as **'Jesus'** and 'The Praying Mantis,' Coupeville, environmental activist
Evelyn Langston – Bellevue, Elliott's "Evil" sister

Walter Gibbs – Oak Harbor developer
Patty Gibbs – Walter's sister, Visalia, California
Judy Gibbs – Walter's wife
Velma Bachelor – Patty's elderly neighbor in Visalia

Marlene Meyers – former county commissioner, now living in Tulare, California and running for state senate
Larry Ward – Right-wing activist, Oak Harbor
Ryan Ashford – 'Chesterfield Man,' paramilitary
Louise (Kristoferson) (Ashford) Moeller – Ashford's ex-wife, living on Camano Island
Dennis Delaney – Ashford's associate, ex CIA contractor, later an Oregon rancher
Alicia Delaney – Dennis' wife, ex CIA informant, Nicaragua
Marvin Trammel – Elliott's neighbor, gravel contractor
Christy Morris – missing high school student, 1965

Ma (Kate) Barker – Owner of Barker Logging Company
R.P. Beath – Citizens Patrol volunteer, ex state legislator

Foreword

When human bones began turning up in 2011 during a street project in Oak Harbor's Old Town, they brought work to a halt. Authorities from the state Department of Archaeology and Historic Preservation determined the bones were from multiple individuals, and that the street probably lay upon a Native American burial ground.

For hundreds of years before Euro-American settlers arrived, the waterfront of Oak Harbor Bay was the site of an indigenous village of the Lower Skagit peoples. They traded and intermarried with other bands throughout the region. When Washington's territorial governor forced the natives to sign treaties in 1855, giving up their land, the natives were relocated to the Swinomish Reservation at LaConner. But the bones of their ancestors remained.

My intention with this book, as with the others in this series, is to take readers to places I love and share the history of Whidbey Island.

This story and all its characters, and their names, are entirely fictional, but the historical context and Salish history are as close to accurate as I can make them. The advantage of fiction in telling a story like this is that it is so personal – the reader can step inside the shoes of a character and imagine what it's like to be them, to see the world through their eyes. It's a way of getting at truth that I think is more immediate than simply recounting events from newspapers and other non-fiction accounts.

Beth Hall, Claire Creighton and my wife, Sue, were the first to read this entire manuscript and give me their comments and recommendations. Beth is a fellow author and serves as my developmental editor when I get down toward the completion of a book. Claire is an avid reader who knows me well from hours of walking and discussing ideas.

Without their help this story would be riddled with errors and inconsistencies.

I met Beth and Claire over the years as we walked our dogs in Langley, in the early morning. My dog *Duncan* thought they'd make good friends, and a dog knows.

As the author, I continued to revise and rearrange content right up till the last. So any errors that remain are my own, likely introduced at the very last moment.

FINAL COVER-UP

DAN PEDERSEN

Time Immemorial

Archaeologist Donald Mosier dug in his pocket for his car keys. He was standing in the parking lot of the Oak Harbor Public Library, taking in the view. To the west lay Pioneer Avenue, with its cafes, boutiques and gift shops. On the hillside behind him, across a chain link fence, sprawled cookie-cutter Navy housing that looked old and tired. To the south, he could see the Navy Exchange, acres of asphalt, and Oak Harbor Marina.

But in his mind, that wasn't the view at all. He was looking back two centuries at a prairie of grasslands on rolling hills, running down to the sparkling waters of the bay.

Golden grasses shimmered in the summer breeze. Here and there, clusters of oak trees spread their broad canopies over the savannah. Meadowlarks sang and pecked at the ground for insects. Butterflies fluttered among tiny wildflowers, and a Blacktail doe and her two spotted fawns grazed in the dappled shade of the leafy canopy.

The archaeologist could still pick out a few remnants of this habitat here in the oldest part of Oak Harbor, on Whidbey Island – a few scraps of tall grass behind the Navy fence, a stunted oak squeezed into some forgotten corner, next to a wood-frame house with peeling paint and a children's swing set. The oaks grew before there was a street here, before conifers, before the Navy and its Whidbey Island base, before the arrival of immigrant settlers and their farms.

One last grove of oaks still stood in this part of town – about a hundred fifty in Smith Park – part of what once had been an expanse that was the defining character of this place.

Mosier closed his eyes and visualized children playing by longhouses where extended families lived under one roof. Salish women cooked over open fires. From time to time, they carried reed baskets full of shells and salmon scraps to the midden at the water's edge and upended them, as their ancestors had done for hundreds of years. Naturally-occurring wildfires and deliberate burning by the Salish cleared the low brush and perpetuated the grasslands, which grew camas flowers, bracken ferns and chocolate lilies, which, in turn, attracted deer and elk, making for easy hunting.

In the bay, paddles flashed as Salish pullers guided their dugout canoes back and forth to neighboring villages at Crescent Harbor and Penn Cove, and the Skagit River delta, where they traded and visited with relatives. The various bands were united by intermarriage, not by any formal leadership structure.

Specialists divvied up the community's work – fishing, hunting, making tools, building canoes and harvesting roots and berries. They lived and worked in the close presence of their deceased ancestors, whose remains were preserved in canoes hung from trees or poles. It was a spectacularly successful, stable and abundant lifestyle that had sustained these people for centuries. But the Salish didn't measure time in the Western way; they just said they had lived here since time immemorial. And they didn't own the land; it belonged to all.

Now, as Mosier beheld a large sinkhole in the

street before him, he supposed another piece of Salish culture was about to be lost, another final resting place destroyed by the bad luck to be located just beneath the street in the middle of what was now the conquering culture's "historic Old Town."

Old? He didn't even know where to start on that idea.

Bones

Sheriff's Deputy Katarina Brown stared down into the mud pit. Water had stopped flowing into the sinkhole since the city shut off the broken main under the street, but the gravel and seepage at the bottom of the hole looked like a deathtrap. If she climbed down there, would she be able to climb back out, or would it just swallow her up?

"Are you sure you want to do this?" asked Don Mosier, the archaeologist, pushing his round bifocal spectacles higher on his nose. "I'm used to it, but I'd sure hate to send you down there. We could do some digging with the excavator and bring up whatever's there to examine in the street."

Kat loved this guy – gentle and soft-spoken, and a science nerd like her. With his gray beard and safari hat, and his trademark khakis, the middle-aged archaeologist looked like he'd just come off the job at Olduvai Gorge in Tanzania.

Blue jeans and a checkered shirt might be more in keeping with the local look, but she suspected the safari get-up was calculated on his part, to telegraph his credentials.

Kat knew darn well that archaeologists don't dig with a steam shovel. She'd watched enough TV to know they worked with their faces a few inches from the remains, finessing the earth away lightly with a soft brush. She also knew Mosier had already developed some hunches about this particular discovery, which was why he wasn't more protective of the cultural aspects.

"Well, you made it down and back alive," Kat said. "I'd like to take a closer look myself before we disturb things any more." She strapped herself into a harness and roped it off to the tracked excavator. "Tell that guy to reel me up fast if I start to sink into the muck," she said, nodding to the machine's operator. The operator touched the brim of his hat to signal that he understood.

Friday evening, when Mosier got the call about the street collapse from Public Works, he had been binge-watching *Time Team*, a British TV series about twenty years of archaeological digs in the United Kingdom. The archaeologists on that show had grown old doing what they loved. He knew them all like old friends.

Mosier was aware that earlier in the week, a spiderweb of cracks had appeared in one of the Old Town intersections. A minor road repair would be needed. But by Sunday morning, the cracks had become a sinkhole twenty feet across and twenty feet deep. A water main that passed under the street apparently had been broken for some time, undermining the pavement.

Now, with a puff of black diesel smoke, a tracked shovel was lowering its bucket into the hole, clawing away gravel from a culvert that had collapsed and needed to come out.

Ever since the city had dug up several sets of Native American remains a few years ago, it was standard procedure to involve Mosier in every dig. And as soon as he looked into the hole, he knew this was going to get complicated.

"Hold it!" Mosier yelled, waving both arms at the machine operator. "Hold up!"

Toward the bottom of the hole, something brown and white, several feet long, protruded from the gravel at the side. It could be an old tree root or a mammoth tusk, but he'd seen enough human bones to know another when he saw it – a femur, the longest bone in the body, a leg bone.

"Shut 'er down," Mosier spoke into his walkie-talkie. "I've to call the tribe. Let's get this whole area cordoned off."

It was Mosier who made the initial descent into the hole right after that and concluded something about the bone wasn't right. Maybe they didn't need the tribe after all.

Discovery of human remains in this part of town was perplexing because this was outside the area where previous Lower Skagit burials had been found. About five blocks away, the city had disturbed a major burial site during an earlier street project. The resulting uproar with local tribes had been a black mark against the city, resulting in the creation of Mosier's position.

All Native American remains now were turned over to the Swinomish community for reburial in the tribal cemetery in LaConner, since the lower Skagits were part of that reservation and Oak Harbor had been the site of a Lower Skagit village.

What many people didn't understand, but Mosier did, was that an advanced civilization of Salish peoples had lived in Oak Harbor for something like fifteen hundred years before any white people. They had come here from the interior before Washington became a state, possibly following the Skagit River downstream.

As recently as ten thousand years ago, toward the end of the ice age in Puget Sound, mammoths and mastodons roamed the area that is now Whidbey Island, and their tusks were periodically found in island bluffs. Chunks of ivory occasionally fell to the beach from nearby cliffs as sediments eroded. Native peoples on the Olympic Peninsula hunted them, as was confirmed at the Manis Mastodon Site near Sequim, where a spearpoint was found embedded in a rib bone. History here went way back, and it gave up its secrets reluctantly.

As the ice retreated, sea levels rose, so the position of the shoreline all over Puget Sound kept changing. But humans soon established villages and shared the island with a large population of wolves. Human habitation did not begin with "discovery" of this paradise on Earth by European-American settlers in the 1850s. The occupation of this land by settlers was a recent postscript, and they had radically changed it. Human occupation went back much, much further, and Mosier's job was to help preserve and respect the culture of those first peoples and the remains of their ancestors.

Much as he loved the native history of this place, this latest bone didn't strike him as Native American. Aside from the unexpected location of the femur, it did not look hundreds or thousands of years old. It was surprisingly white and fresh, and it was long. Mosier had never seen a Salish native as tall as this.

Just to cover the bases, he called the city police and they called the sheriff's department. The sheriff sent Kat Brown, an especially resourceful officer who had become their lead homicide investigator alongside her mentor, Shane Lindstrom.

Kat tested her rope and then descended over the edge of the pit toward the protruding bone. Chunks of earth and rock broke loose and tumbled alongside her to the bottom.

She reached the bone and was just starting to examine it when she looked down at the shifting earth below her. She was standing inches from an eerie set of white teeth. It was a skull – make that two skulls, complete with jawbones and eye sockets. When she bent down for a closer look, she could see each skull had a hole the size of a quarter in the back of the cranium.

These didn't look like old bones.

"Don," she yelled back to Mosier, who was standing on the rim. "You'd better have another look at this."

By afternoon, Mosier had removed and photographed the better part of two skeletons lying in a jumbled heap, the bones intermingled. They had not been "buried" but dumped.

He was still finding additional bones, but had enough already to know he was looking at two adult individuals of differing height. Dental work in the jawbones made it clear these were not Native American remains. The teeth would also help him estimate the individuals' ages, and the pelvises would reveal their gender. He suspected he was looking at a man and a woman.

Oak Harbor Police were reviewing their missing persons files, and Kat was doing the same with countywide disappearances. The big question was how far back to look.

"What do you think?" Kat asked Mosier. "Can you take a stab at how long these skeletons have been here?"

"Two thousand eight."

"You're kidding," she said. "You can be that precise? You haven't even started to examine them."

"That was the last time this intersection was dug up," Mosier said. "My guess is that's when someone dumped their bodies here, thinking they'd never be seen again underneath a paved street. Or if they were, that they'd be considered Native American remains."

"How could someone deposit bodies in a downtown intersection without being observed?" Kat asked.

"That's tricky," Mosier said, "but this is not the busiest part of town. Traffic would have been detoured away from here when the street was dug up. The bodies could have been left here at night when no one was around, or they could have been in a truckload of gravel that was delivered to the site. If that was the case, I can't imagine the driver didn't know what he was carrying. After dumping the load, he'd want to make sure the bodies weren't visible on the surface. If they were, he'd have to go down in the hole with a shovel and cover them up."

"Have you found any artifacts with them – rings, clothing, personal items?"

"None at all. I think the bodies were nude when they went into the ground, but we'll keep looking."

"And the cause of death?"

"Oh, homicide – a single gunshot to the back of the head in each case. I haven't found any other injuries on the bones up to this point except compaction from the gravel overburden, but again, we'll keep looking and we'll see what the medical examiner says."

Going Back

So far, Oak Harbor Police were coming up with nothing. They had no simultaneous disappearances in 2008 of two individuals. In fact, there were no such disappearances in the city's police files going back decades, though Kat knew it was possible the victims might be unrelated and unconnected to each other.

But when Kat dug into the county's files, she found a 2008 case that intrigued her.

Elliott Langston of Coupeville had disappeared from his mobile home in November of that year. He was a prominent environmental activist and lived in a secluded patch of woods on five acres just out of town.

He was such a controversial figure, and disappeared so mysteriously, Kat had a feeling he could be one of the skeletons in the hole. But who was the other person? She was a total mystery. Maybe Kat could find more information in newspaper accounts from that time. She turned to her computer and scrolled through the newspaper's digital archives. In late November, 2008, she found the article she was looking for:

Police Seek Public's Help In Lawyer's Disappearance

Sheriff's deputies are asking for help in the disappearance of a prominent lawyer and environmental activist from Coupeville.

Elliott Langston was last seen November 28 when he left a county hearing on whether to approve a 280-acre housing development west of Oak Harbor.

When he failed to return phone calls or to appear at several subsequent county hearings where he was expected to testify, sheriff's deputies visited his mobile home and found his truck parked in front of it, but no sign of Langston. There was no evidence of foul play. Nothing was missing, and there has been no activity in his bank account or credit cards.

"There is simply no evidence of a crime," said Sheriff's Deputy Roger Gray, "but the circumstances of his disappearance are highly suspicious. It appears he told no one he was planning to be away. At this point our investigation is at a standstill, unless or until new evidence comes to light."

Kat knew Deputy Roger Gray well. He was an old friend in the department – as old as any of Kat's relationships went, given that she was one of the youngest deputies in the department and he was the oldest before his retirement two years ago.

She knew where to find him, likely fishing at Possession Point with his lab, *Midnight*. She still had his cell phone number in her contacts, and dialed it. He apparently had her programmed into his contacts, also, because he answered, "Kat, sweetheart, this is a welcome surprise."

"Awwww, you're such a flirt in your declining years. I was just calling because I've missed *Midnight*."

"You want to talk to him?" Roger asked.

"Yes, please."

"Hang on and I'll put him on speaker phone," Roger said. "I may have to howl a little to get him started."

"I'm looking forward to it."

Kat held the phone away from her ear as Roger

started some high-pitched wailing. He had told her labs are not generally known as "howling" breeds, not like Huskies, for example, but they'll often respond to a siren. Pretty soon *Midnight* joined in, howling dolefully from someplace deep and primal in his soul.

"My god, I've got goosebumps," Kat said. "That's like no other sound on earth."

"I know. I'm getting looks from the other boats out here. When he sings it's like he goes back thousands of years to someplace in his soul. But I suppose you have a business reason for this call."

"Yes, I'm afraid I do. Where the heck are you, by the way?"

"About a quarter mile off Scatchet Head."

"Could we talk when you get back? I need some information about a cold case."

"Which one?"

"Elliott Langston."

After a moment's silence, Roger replied, "I'm not doing much good out here this morning, so if you'd like to meet at the launch ramp, I can be there in about half-an-hour."

*

Kat got to the ramp early and was waiting when Roger's boat pulled into view in the bay. *Midnight* was sitting up in the bow and barked twice when he saw Kat sitting on a log on the beach. On a perfect summer day, with a gentle breeze and just a few white clouds in a blue sky, this didn't seem much like working.

Roger brought the boat up alongside the pier and *Midnight* hopped off and ran to Kat. After saying her proper hellos to the dog, Kat helped Roger stow his gear in his truck and reel the boat onto its trailer. Roger pulled his rig out of the way in the parking lot and then walked back to join Kat on the beach.

"So, what's on your mind?" he asked.

"Elliott Langston. What can you tell me about him?"

"The Praying Mantis," Roger said. "That's what they called him because he was so darn tall and lanky, and his trademark pose of leaning forward on his two elbows while he listened. He'd sit in county hearings quietly, not moving a muscle, till he caught a contradiction in something you said, and then he'd bite your head off. I can tell you almost anything except why he disappeared. Is there a break in the case?"

"Possibly," Kat said. "We've got a pair of skeletons and will know more after we look at dental records."

"Pair? That was one of the strangest cases I ever investigated. Langston was here one day and gone the next. There was absolutely no evidence of foul play, but I always believed he was murdered. If it was murder, it was a professional job – the killer left no trace."

"Who was on your list of suspects?"

"Well initially, it was his sister, Evelyn, in Medina. He pronounced her name *Evil*yn. They were in an ugly fight over an inheritance their mother left exclusively to Evelyn. She was her mother's caregiver in her final years, and Elliott was feuding with her and also with his late father. Elliott was estranged from them all. They were all conservative Republicans and, after college, he became an antiwar liberal. That was one thing, but he also strongly objected to how his father accumulated his wealth, and was furious at the end about being cut out of the will. His sister and her husband inherited a fortune."

"Did you interview her?" Kat asked.

"I sure did. Elliott and Evelyn were never close, and shortly before he disappeared, they were going at each other tooth-and-nail with legal maneuvering, but I could never come up with a good reason for her to arrange his death. She was holding the winning cards."

He added. "A lot of people hated Elliott but he had some legitimate grievances against her and their parents. They made their money by conning senior citizens out of their land at grossly undervalued prices. It wasn't strictly illegal, just unethical.

"My neighbor received countless offers from them to buy his five forested acres for $33,000 cash, when its actual fair market value was about $165,000. Some people were so addled and desperate in their old age they accepted these offers without even bothering to research them. Mind you, decades earlier they had probably bought the land for one or two thousand dollars, so $33,000 sounded like a windfall."

Kat nodded, and Roger continued. "He had dozens of enemies here in the county. He was a brilliant environmental lawyer who blocked or tied up just about every permit application that came along, but his bedside manner left something to be desired. At the time of his disappearance, he was raising legal hurdles to stop annexation of a large parcel of farmland outside Oak Harbor for a new housing development. Millions of dollars were on the line. He looked like a country bumpkin but was extremely sharp. You didn't want to go against him."

"I'm sure you dug into that development project," Kat said.

"I did, but it was only one of many projects where he stepped on someone's toes. And keep in mind, we didn't have a body – or anything."

"Well, that sounds like more than enough motive to make him go away."

"I always thought so, but don't forget his neighbor here in Coupeville."

"What neighbor?"

"Marvin Trammel. He was on awful terms with Elliott over the way he kept his property. Trammel said he was driving down property values in his end of town and was the reason he couldn't sell his land – nobody wanted to live next to him. Whoever bought that land would never be able to cut a tree without a lawsuit. Elliott would find an eagle's nest on it and that would be the end of it."

Roger sat back and stroked his beard. "Have you looked at his property?"

"Not yet. I don't even have proof yet that it was Elliott's skeleton in the hole."

"Take a look," Roger said. "Evelyn has let it sit all this time as a sort of sick shrine to her brother. Maybe she didn't want to touch it in case he came back and slapped another lawsuit against her."

"I assume you searched thoroughly.

"Inside and out, with a fine-toothed comb. There was nothing in the house. Elliott was not much of a housekeeper – the place was a mess of boxes, papers, dishes. One odd thing I noticed was that the guest room was very neat – the neatest room in the house."

"That's curious.

"Yes. Maybe he was expecting a guest, or maybe it was just a thing with him to keep the guest room ready at all times. Those spare rooms in people's houses often end up as junk rooms. Elliott didn't seem the type to have guests. Mostly, I was focused on the outside, hoping to get lucky and find shell casings. About fifty yards down the driveway I did find some tire prints and a couple of cigarette butts. They may or may not have meant something."

"Do you remember the brand?"

"Geez, Kat! Off the top of my head, I'm going to say Chesterfield. By the way, Elliott was not a smoker, for what it's worth. At one point I even wondered if he might be buried on the property. We brought in a cadaver dog and searched for places where the earth had been disturbed, but found nothing."

Kat's mind was racing, "I think I'll drive over there now."

FINAL COVER-UP

Long driveways and roads in the woods often held secrets, she knew. Unlike the city, where the houses were lined up side-by-side and visible to their neighbors and passersby, homes in the woods were intensely private and individual. One homeowner might carve out a dream home in the trees while the people just out of sight, next door, lived in squalor like hillbillies. No one ever knew the story of these hidden neighborhoods unless invited to visit. The sheriff and first responders typically found out only when called to handle an emergency.

The advent of Google Earth had given law enforcement a new tool to at least get a sense of what they would find when they drove up some of these roads. Kat often relied on it as the first step in her research, and that's what she did this time, too, before turning up Elliott Langston's drive. Still, it didn't convey the full impact of what she would find.

"Positively No Trespassing," stated the faded yellow sign with the skull and crossbones at the entrance to Elliott Langston's property. It was anchored by two sturdy four-by-four posts. *"Private Road. Unlawful to Enter. No Entrance to Trammel Residence. Violators Will Be Prosecuted."*

Kat scratched her head. If there was some dispute between the two neighbors and Trammel was not allowed to use this shared access road, then how could he reach his own property? Had Langston put up the sign to torment his neighbor?

Kat was shocked when she saw Langston's mobile home. It was posted "Sheriff's Line: Do Not Cross," but vandals had pelted it with rocks, broken all the windows and ripped the door off its hinges. Kat could smell rats before she saw them.

This was a public health hazard. She was not going inside without a respirator, and did not have one with her. But one look at the situation told her much of what she needed to know. Even without the rats and the vandalism, this would be a junk heap. She looked around at the scene, then got into her cruiser and backtracked several hundred yards to the turnoff to the Trammel property.

By contrast, the Trammel home was beautiful. It was a cedar Northwest contemporary in a wooded setting, with manicured landscaping, a lush chemical lawn, skylights and a tidy woodpile. The whole yard was surrounded by hybrid rhododendrons, and the centerpiece was a rose garden. Someone here loved gardening. It crossed her mind that Langston, an environmentalist, would have cringed at the use of weed killers and fertilizers that poison the water table and kill bees and birds.

Kat knew there were conflicting philosophies on the island about landscaping. Some people approached it with a "city vision" of what a perfect yard should look like. In time, most came to see perfection in a different way – in maintaining a healthy environment for wildlife, pets and humans, free of poisons. You could spot them by the dandelions and buttercups in their lawns. Langston was one of the dandelion people.

In the manicured back yard of Trammel's home were a colorful swing set and slide, a play area for grandchildren, Kat assumed.

Parked next to a tall aluminum outbuilding was a gravel truck with a flatbed lowboy trailer behind it, with a "Trammel Excavating" backhoe on board.

A very fit gentleman in a flannel shirt was swinging an axe, splitting firewood – Marvin Trammel, she supposed.

She watched his eyes follow her as she pulled into the driveway and parked on clean pea gravel behind his green Toyota land cruiser. Before she could open the door to get out of her vehicle, he put down his axe and walked her way. His shoes crunched on the loose gravel.

"Good afternoon, officer," he greeted. "What can I do for you?"

Kat opened her door, got out and stood by her car.

"I've just been next door taking a look at things," Kat said.

Trammel glanced down at his shoes and shook his head. "Has Elliott come back from the dead to sue me about the road?" he laughed.

"What makes you assume he's dead?"

"No one has seen him since 2008. Where else could he be?"

Kat didn't answer. "I noticed the sign about the road. I take it you and Elliott didn't have a very cordial relationship."

Trammel leaned back and laughed. "You think? I asked him nicely to clean up his property but he would have none of it. He didn't like the way I kept mine. The access road was an endless bone of contention. He refused to spend any money to maintain it."

"Were there any threats back and forth about it?" Kat asked.

"Not in so many words. I went to the county and lodged a complaint. After that, he filed a lawsuit challenging the recorded easement that gave me the right to use the road. I was never so happy in my life as when he just disappeared off the face of the earth."

"Any idea who would have wanted him gone?"

"Everyone."

Wetland

County Commissioner Marlene Meyers stood just inside the door at the back of the room and watched as the hearing examiner recognized Elliott Langston and invited him to speak. It was the week before Thanksgiving of 2008. More and more, it looked like The Gibbs Addition to the City of Oak Harbor was hopelessly stalled. If Langston succeeded in blocking it, two-hundred-fifty homes would never be built. Investors would be sitting on unbuildable land worth only a fraction of what had been spent on this project already.

"Mr. Examiner," Langston began, unfolding his long body from his chair and brushing his hair away from his face. He looked around the room. Aside from the hearing examiner behind the podium, the audience was several representatives of Gibbs Development Corporation and about two dozen landowners Meyers recognized, who lived within the proposed rezone.

"This application," Langston said, "holding aloft a fistful of paperwork, "is based on a complete distortion of the historical record and bad science. The area described has been mined off-and-on for eighty-three years as a peat bog. The Lower Skagits harvested berries here as far back as we can see. It is full of native plant species we associate with a moist environment." He put down the application, picked up another document, paused and turned the page of his notes.

"It borders a marsh on the west, and any development will deplete valuable nesting habitat for wildlife. But what should especially concern property owners is that it will divert surface-water runoff, causing the flooding of homes to the north. It should never have been considered for homesites. I have here the applicant's own original environmental impact assessment, which has been altered to remove references to freshwater marine life and moisture-dependent native plants and shrubs growing on the property." Langston turned and looked momentarily at Meyers.

"You're suggesting the applicant deliberately altered ..." the examiner asked, leaning forward and pulling the microphone closer in the hearing room. He also cast a glance at Myers.

"I'm not saying who did it, but it's a stunning omission," Langston replied. "I can only conclude someone deliberately falsified the information. I've walked the property, taken photographs and identified a list of classic wetland species and indicators, which I'd like to submit for your consideration." He handed the file to the hearing examiner, who took a moment to flip through the pages.

"This looks quite detailed. In light of what Mr. Langston has presented," the examiner said, looking up at the audience, "I'm going to suspend this hearing to study these materials. We'll take up this request again in a week."

Hands shot up in the audience. "Does this mean the sale of my property is off?" one man shouted to the hearing examiner, who ignored the question.

"What just happened?" asked an older woman.

"Well, this is a mess," Langston heard someone else say. "Now what?"

Langston turned, closed his briefcase, and headed for the exit. Meyers was already gone.

Last Will
Months Earlier

"She did *what?*" Elliott Langston asked, raising his voice to a high-pitched whine and twisting his face.

"She left everything to me. See for yourself," the woman said, handing the man a photocopied document titled, 'Last Will and Testament.'"

He flipped several pages till he found the words, "house and all other assets."

"I'm giving you the courtesy of letting you know now, so you won't get blindsided by the lawyer."

"Courtesy?" he asked. "*Courtesy?* This is highway robbery."

"It was Mother's last wish."

"It was a brilliant con on your part. She was not in her right mind. You know that."

They were standing in the home's foyer in Medina, east of Seattle's Lake Washington. The man's prim sister, Evelyn, hadn't even invited him to sit at the table, and in light of this, he wouldn't do it even if invited.

With his shoulder-length Jesus hair, ragged blond beard and torn blue denim shirt, Elliott Langston looked like he'd slept on the street. His 1990 Toyota truck, with its mismatched fender and dented hood, sat directly in front of the Victorian-style brick home with its manicured lawn, stone archway, courtyard and fountain, and Evelyn's black BMW.

Langston had driven here to meet with Evelyn after their mother's death. They had never been close. After high school, Langston had gone off to the university, where professors challenged his mind to think about the world's social problems. Evelyn had attended community college on the east side of Lake Washington and married a corporate accountant named Justin, whom Elliott detested.

"You won't get away with this," Elliott snarled. "I'll see you in court."

"Fine, for all the good it will do you," Evelyn said. "Where were you the last four years while I cared for Mother night and day? She knew who loved her and who just wanted her money."

The comment stung. It was dirty money but Langston could do a lot of good with it.

"As if there was an iota of love in her," Langston said. "She was a greedy old woman who lived in luxury by exploiting hundreds of elderly people who sold their land to Dad for a pittance of its value."

"She and Daddy were good business people. Thanks to them, people got fast cash for their wooded acreage at a stage of life when the land was just a burden to them."

"She and Daddy were blood suckers. You know it as well as I do."

Elliott had come to this realization in high school and it had only grown at the University of Washington. His dad had never been affectionate, never hugged or said, "I love you." In Elliott's mind it was symptomatic of a much greater disconnect in his dad's humanity altogether. He simply had no feeling for others – only for what he could gain from them.

This was clear the closer he drew to high school graduation. His entire future, possibly whether he lived or died, would be determined by a lottery conducted by the Selective Service System. His dad really didn't care one way or the other.

Money and connections, and private clubs, were how his dad operated. Anything that expanded business opportunities was good. Anything that reduced them was bad. War was good for the economy. Social justice just got in the way.

The kids in this rich enclave all benefited from privilege, whether they realized it or not. But the lottery forced them to make life-changing decisions before they were ready. If their lottery numbers were low and they were drafted into the army, they would almost certainly join nearly three million Americans to serve in Vietnam. Tens of thousands already had died in that faraway place, and for what?

Elliott's dad thought the military would actually do his son good. "You have no direction in life. You need structure." Some of his classmates strongly felt the war was immoral. If he served in the military, they might forever see him as morally weak. Others felt it was their patriotic duty to go.

He could move to Canada or declare he was a conscientious objector. Would that be more courageous, or less, than allowing himself to be drafted? He didn't think he qualified for a medical exemption. His best option was to stay in school, enroll in college, and hope the war would be over by the time he completed his studies. The Selective Service System allowed students time to complete their education. With a little luck, he could go on with his life as if Vietnam had never happened.

University

Head down, arms weighted with books, Langston walked the length of the University of Washington Quadrangle. The Quad, a network of sidewalks across a central green plaza, was his favorite shortcut to the library. It was rimmed on all sides by classic Gothic buildings. Generations of students had climbed the steps to those buildings. He couldn't put the feeling into words, but the architecture here conveyed a timelessness, a sense that he was part of something greater than himself, more important and universal than just his own education.

On this March afternoon, The Quad was the most beautiful he had seen it, awash in pink, with dozens of cherry trees in peak bloom. It was good to be alive.

*

"We can do better," Robert F. Kennedy declared. Langston leaned left and right to see over the crowd as thousands of students broke into applause. "There are no easy solutions to the strife at home to our course in Vietnam, but there are ways we can do better."

Langston had heard about Kennedy's visit to the university by chance a few hours earlier and decided on impulse to attend. With President Johnson declining to run for reelection, Kennedy had declared his own candidacy just ten days earlier. He struck Langston as young but refreshing, a contemporary from his own generation, not another old man with old ideas.

More and more, Kat was sure one of the bodies under the street was Elliott Langston, based on the timing of his disappearance and the street repair. Her process when investigating a murder was to learn as much as she could about the victim – how they lived, what they thought, and what might have brought them into conflict with someone else.
She knew Elliott Langston had attended the University of Washington after graduating from high school in the wealthy East Side suburb of Medina. No doubt the university had shaped his anti-establishment values, which were out of synch with the pro-war attitudes of a military community like Oak Harbor.
The 1960s and 70s, the Vietnam era, were before her time, but a few hours of reading online gave her a picture of Elliott's world when he was still a student. Kat's friend, retired deputy Roger Gray, had lived through that decade and added a more personal perspective from his own experience, and also shared what he had learned about Langston's university years during his initial investigation, years ago.
Langston had been part of the nation's first-ever "freeway march" by student anti-war protesters in 1970. It took place at his school, the University of Washington.
For young men just out of high school, the 1970s were complicated. The more Kat read about those years, the better she understood the anguish many students felt, and how they had become radicalized on both sides of the political divide – some going to Asia to fight what they believed was a patriotic war against Communism, and others bombing ROTC buildings to

fight *against* that war for patriotic reasons right here at home.

Elliott had rejected his parents' values and become estranged from them while at the university. She closed her eyes and let her imagination go. She might not have every detail right, but believed she understood much of what had shaped Langston and other young people into the activists they'd become.

*

Langston sat cross-legged in the northbound lanes of Interstate Highway 5, just south of the Northeast Forty-Fifth Street overpass in Seattle's University District. It was an uncommonly beautiful day and he couldn't help thinking how surreal it was to be sitting here on the pavement where thousands of cars normally roared past every day.

His mind wandered and he pictured Joel McIntosh, a high school classmate, sitting on the ground somewhere in the jungles of Vietnam, praying he'd survive the next patrol down a booby-trapped trail. Everyone had a classmate who had gone to Vietnam, and some already had returned in body bags. Others had returned psychologically damaged, addicted to mind-numbing drugs, unable to function in normal society or hold a job.

This was the great watershed after high school – you went from childhood, overnight, to either the best years of your life or the worst. For most young men, there was no third option. There was no taking a year off to think about what you wanted to do with your life. You needed a survival strategy and Elliott's classmates found it through student deferments, physical exemptions, conscientious objection or enlisting in a branch that did not generally send kids to a war zone during their first term, such as the Air Force.

Behind Langston, about three thousand more students stood or sat, blocking the northbound lanes to all traffic. He didn't know how many had gathered that morning in front of the student union building but surely thousands, of whom maybe half had continued on to the freeway. They had come together to hear speakers try to make sense of the killing of four Kent State University students the previous day by National Guard troops on the Ohio campus.

The Kent State students had been attending a rally opposing expansion of the Vietnam War into Cambodia. Tension, violence and the threat of violence were running high. Elliott and the other UW students wanted to show support for them, to march somewhere and make their feelings visible.

Langston was furious, full of grief and outrage about what had happened at Kent State. If students could be shot there, they could be shot anywhere, on any campus, including here. Until now, no one thought being a student was life-threatening. Those Kent State students had gotten up that morning, never imagining in their wildest dreams they wouldn't live to see the end of the day – that they could be shot and killed on an American college campus by a frightened American soldier.

After presenting a list of demands to university president Charles Odegaard that included banning the National Guard and Reserve Officer Training Corps (ROTC) from the UW campus, the Seattle students had marched several blocks to the freeway. No one knew their plan, and probably there wasn't any. The idea of marching onto the freeway seemed to come spontaneously from someone in the crowd who shouted, "Onto the freeway."

Facing them, some thirty Seattle police officers with white helmets and nightsticks formed a laughably thin human barricade across all three lanes of the mainline, and the express lane.

FINAL COVER-UP

Langston had awakened that morning in McMahon Hall, an eleven-story dormitory centered around twin towers on north campus. It catered to serious upper classmen and grad students. Langston had no idea he would wind up in this place today, doing this.

As a law student, Langston lived in a coveted single-occupancy room in one of McMahon's clusters, groupings of four rooms around a common lounge sharing a bathroom. The lounge had a refrigerator, a balcony, some vinyl furniture and a TV. Cluster living was the most enlightened concept in student housing at the UW, though Langston laughed when he saw McMahon's minimalist concrete architecture described as "brutalist." It didn't seem minimalist or brutal to him – he had a million-dollar view of Lake Washington.

Clustermates called him a geek and that didn't bother him at all. Half the students in McMahon were eccentric. One guy, known as the California Sun God, ate only peas for dinner – no one knew why. He spent hours sunbathing on the building's ground-level terrace in full view of hundreds of coed residents, even on the coldest winter days. It was what passed as normal here.

With Langston's long hair and neglect of his personal appearance, he was just one more odd duck. His plan was to go into environmental law. He had chosen the environment partly as a way of getting back at his parents, who had devoted their life's work to exploiting it for gain.

"Jesus, you've risen from the dead," one of his clustermates remarked as Langston staggered half-asleep to the bathroom in his underwear. It was Fadhian Singh, a wealthy foreign student from Bombay, smoking a rancid Dunhill cigarette. Fadhain missed no opportunity to remind them that his name meant "a gift from God." He seemed to think his aristocratic status from home carried over to student living. He called Langston "Jesus" because of his long hair. Langston didn't like him. Fadhian made no secret that his plan was to marry an American girl, become a citizen, and stay in the U.S. Langston couldn't imagine any co-ed naïve enough to be taken in by this obnoxious egotist.

Another clustermate, Terry, was studying to become a cop and working as a police cadet. He wore a police uniform and carried a sidearm – nice guy, but Langston couldn't get used to seeing that gun in a student dorm. Terry had a habit of slinging the gun and holster over the chair at his desk and leaving the door open to the lounge while he took a shower. Langston wondered where Terry stood when it came to all the anti-war sentiment on campus. Was he sympathetic, or full of anger at his fellow students? He didn't say much about it.

There was a New Yorker, Abraham, studying forestry. He said he was from "Long Guyland." He had more than the usual body hair and everyone ribbed him about his long guylashes. The clustermates were an odd mix of loners. Langston found it hard to generalize about them politically. Like him, they were just trying to hold onto their military deferments and get on with their lives.

He had never been much involved in campus politics and expected to spend this day in the library, studying. But he had taken some history and political science courses from prominent liberal professors. When he finished school, he knew he would face the draft and possibly a tour in Vietnam, which was beyond imagination. He never expected the war to last this long.

Events in Southeast Asia hung over everything, and Langston kept expecting something to give. He couldn't imagine what would cause American soldiers, kids his own age, to slaughter five hundred Vietnamese civilians in the 1968 Me Lai Massacre.

Was that what American had become, what people like his father believed patriotism was about? If he were drafted, would he become a murderer, too?

Events were spinning out of control. President John F. Kennedy was assassinated in 1963. Then in 1968, Rev. Martin Luther King Jr., was assassinated in April and Robert F. Kennedy in June. Not only was the war tearing the country apart, so was the struggle for social justice – Civil Rights. It was impossible not to take sides and be swept up in these issues, especially for college students.

In January, 1968, North Vietnam launched the Tet Offensive against major cities in the south. US forces suffered heavy losses, badly undermining support for the war at home. The CBS News anchorman, Walter Cronkite, shocked Middle America when he declared the war unwinnable and headed for a stalemate.

Elliott imagined his dad watching Cronkite speak those words, which must have shaken everything he believed. Hard-liner Richard Nixon won the presidency, defeating anti-war Democrat Hubert Humphrey, and saying he had a secret plan to end the war. The secret seemed to be making it larger. Elliott felt trapped. Everything was looking worse and worse.

If he could stay out of Vietnam, he knew where he would move when he finished school – to Whidbey Island. It was close to Seattle, defined by water, an accident of geography that was anything but cohesive when it came to values. Politics, patriotism, noise and the environment generated constant friction between north and south.

The south and central regions were rural, much of the land still forested or tilled for crops. The fields were pleasing to the eye. The people were older and embraced nature and a quiet lifestyle, and the intimacy of village life, which they found in Langley and Coupeville. To Langston, this part of the island was idyllic. There were sandy beaches and walking trails, farms and lakes, and acres of prairie.

The north was more urban, dominated by a large Navy base and a young demographic that favored box stores, fast cars and fast food, and loud airplanes. With the government pumping money and jobs into the North Whidbey economy, developers saw almost unlimited opportunities for profit.

This island, with its warring camps, was the perfect setting for an environmental lawyer.

New School
1964

The white, two-door BMW luxury coupe pulled to a stop directly in front of the school. Marlene Meyers's mother, behind the wheel, turned and remarked, "I wish you wouldn't use so much perfume – a little goes a long way. Are you sure you've got everything?"

"Yes, Mom," Marlene said, opening the passenger door. "See you later." She grabbed a notebook full of blank paper and opened the door.

Marlene stood by the car for a moment and watched her new classmates converge on the main building. She already knew boys were looking at her. *Who's the new girl?* With her long legs, golden tan, mid-back blonde hair and high-buttoned white blouse, she was ready for a grand entrance. She knew with the instinct of a predator how to move – slowly and confidently, head high.

Her new school was nothing like the old one, in Berkeley, where incomes were among the highest in the nation. That was both good and bad. This place might lack the prestige, but in this little town she was instant aristocracy. Her dad, a rear admiral, was the ranking military officer on the island and her mom would soon be the prima donna of the officers' wives club, where she would drink too much and try to hide it. She concealed her weak ego behind flirtatiousness –

was a master at charming the men who came around.

Her mom and dad barely talked to each other. Marlene always felt her mom's job was to be the trophy wife and nothing more, another decoration for her dad's uniform. She was weak and pathetic.

"I hate you!" Marlene screamed when they fought. "Hate, hate, hate!" She chose the words to hurt. "You want to ruin my life, but what have you done with your life? Nothing."

"Someday you'll understand life isn't as simple as you think it is," her mom replied. "It's all about compromise."

Marlene craved her dad's approval. She was *not* her mother – not some decoration for a man. She had set some goals, to run for student body president and become active in campus politics. From there, after graduation, she might go on to public office or a career in business.

Much as she despised her mom's weakness, she had learned some useful skills from her when it came to the opposite sex. Her mom was a traditional Southern belle and had a way of talking to men in a breathless voice, almost a whisper, that drew them closer. Turn that voice loose on a man and he would do anything. The lesson wasn't lost on her.

Larry Ward watched the new girl enter the building. He'd never seen such poise and self-assurance, especially on someone's first day. Whatever it took, he was going to catch her eye. He followed and found her standing in the hall, looking around.

"Are you new?" he asked. "I'm Larry Ward. Anything I can do to help?"

"I'm looking for the office," she replied in a breathless whisper. "I need to get my locker assignment."

"Follow me," he said, leading her through the crowd. "Welcome to Oak Harbor. What year are you?"

"Senior. I'll be out of here in a year," and she laughed. He loved the laugh.

"Me, too," he said. Larry thought she was well developed for her age. "Where did you transfer from?"

"Berkeley."

"Oh, cool," he said. "What do you think of Oak Harbor so far?"

"There's a lot of trees. What do people do here for fun?"

"Go somewhere else." Then he took a big risk.

"Hey, do you want to have lunch with me later in the cafeteria – I mean, so you don't have to sit there alone on your first day?"

"I might," she said in her whisper.

Larry took the "might" as a "yes."

"See you at eleven-thirty."

Missing

"Isn't that shocking?" Marlene asked Larry as they sat on her couch. "I mean about that girl who disappeared."

"Christy Morris? Yeah, I guess so – if she's even missing," Larry said.

"You don't think something bad happened to her?" Marlene asked.

"She might have run away."

"Did you know her?" Marlene asked.

"Not really. I don't think she had a lot of friends."

"Was she unhappy?"

"I don't know. Maybe. Sometimes people seem one way in public, but what goes on in private is different."

"Did she have a boyfriend?"

"I don't know. I don't think so."

"She lived just down the road. Mom and Dad are watching me like hawks now. I can't leave the house after dark."

One of their classmates, a freshman named Christy Morris, had disappeared two weeks ago. At first, no one at school even realized she was gone. She was shy, and Black, and kept mostly to herself. When her parents discovered her missing one morning, they reported it to the police, who said these cases usually resolve themselves in twenty-four hours. After giving her a little more time to turn up, they investigated but developed no good leads. Officers visited the school and talked with some of her classmates and teachers. No one knew her very well and they came up with nothing. She had no known boyfriend.

Larry's stomach hurt and he was finding it hard to sleep. He couldn't believe that, just when things were going so well with Marlene, she wanted to talk about Christy. He had barely been able to think about anything else. He and his three best friends had killed her. It wasn't on purpose. They'd been drinking and had left the scene of an accident. All four had participated in disposing of her body. If anyone found out, their lives were over.

But they had gotten away with it! Larry felt different now. It was possible to kill somebody and just go on with your life.

It had happened just a few hundred feet from where he was sitting right now in Marlene's living room.

If he had realized where Marlene lived, he might have found some reason not to come here today and drive over the very spot where he'd helped Ryan Ashford load the body into his trunk. He looked for skid marks as he drove, but the rain that night had greased the road and washed away any trace. That was an incredibly lucky break. The damage to Ryan's car was minor, just an innocent dent on the right rear quarter panel. This was the first time Marlene had invited him to her home on West Beach Road, overlooking the Strait of Juan de Fuca.

He and Marlene were embracing on the sofa in the front parlor. They had sat down a foot apart so Larry could help Marlene with a geometry question Marlene didn't understand. Larry explained it and Marlene reached out and tapped his arm lightly in her delight.

"Well, that was worthwhile," she laughed flirtatiously, leaving him to wonder exactly what she meant.

He had noticed she was expressive that way – with touch – and Larry slid closer on the sofa. Marlene did not back away. Larry brushed her shoulders with the arm he was resting on the back of the sofa, and she leaned closer. Then, without warning, she turned and kissed him. Now, he knew she was interested in more than just some homework assistance.

Moments later, both of his hands were exploring her back and finding the straps and hooks beneath her blouse. He wasn't about to take anything apart, not in her parents' house. He was just discovering the mysteries of something he'd never experienced before.

On the coffee table in front of them sat several open textbooks, which Larry was pretty sure she had arranged as props in case her parents showed up unexpectedly. On the carpet at Marlene's feet was her lavender book bag. Larry could smell perfume on her neck and hear wind-driven surf crashing on the beach below, at the foot of the bluff. But the loudest sound by far was the thump-thump of his own heart, pounding inside his head.

Right now he was just marveling that he had gotten this far with Marlene at all.

"Mom is at some officers' wives tea," Marlene had announced when Larry delivered her home from school in his car. "I don't know where Dad is, but why don't you come in and keep me company for a while?" she said in her breathless whisper. "It's okay to entertain in the living room." Larry thought the word "entertain" oddly quaint and charming.

They had just finished embracing on the sofa when Larry became aware they were not alone in the house. He felt the admiral's approach in the hall, the vibration of someone walking with purpose, and broke off the kiss before Marlene's dad entered the room.

"Good afternoon," her dad boomed in a baritone. "Studying?" Larry detected some sarcasm in the word.

"Yes, Daddy," Marlene replied, her face red and hair ruffled. "Geometry. I'd like you to meet my friend, Larry, who gave me a ride home."

"Young man," the admiral acknowledged, shaking hands with a grip so tight it sent pain shooting up Walter's arm. He probably did it on purpose.

"Larry is a varsity wrestler and captain of the debate club," Marlene said. Larry sensed the admiral examining him, taking in his all-American crewcut and letter jacket. The admiral smiled. Was he liking what he saw?

"I'm going to run for student body president and Larry is going to be my campaign manager," Marlene announced.

"Well then, you have a lot to discuss. Good luck to you both. I'll leave you to it," he said, turning on his heels and starting to walk out of the room.

Halfway to the door, he stopped. "Take care of my daughter," he said. "I'm a little nervous after that incident with the girl down the road."

"I will, sir, absolutely," Larry replied, sitting up straight.

Marlene's announcement about running for office with Larry as her campaign manager was news to him – the first he had heard about her plans and his own role in them.

*

Larry slammed his locker, spun the combination lock, and merged into the crowd of classmates in the school hallway. He couldn't wipe the smile off his face from yesterday. At seventeen, he was tall and muscular, the son of a Naval officer, and wearing a purple-and-gold letter jacket. He was carrying an armload of books and a three-ring binder with a U.S. flag decal on it, and some pictures of Navy jets and an aircraft carrier.

He *might* have a girlfriend.

Classes were over for the day and he had arranged to meet his wrestling-squad teammates at the store across the street. There was a picnic bench out back where they could talk privately.

"We need to go over some things," he said, taking a sip of his Coke and setting down the can. "First, we all need to keep our mouths shut. I mean really shut. Right now, everything's fine, but if anyone talks, this whole thing will come crashing down on us. If any of us plan to apply to the military academy or have military careers, we have to agree this never happened."

The others nodded.

"Secondly, I think we should get proactive. In this town it's just the smart thing to do."

"What do you mean?" one of the others asked.

"Fly the flag. The more we define ourselves as pro-Navy and all-American, the better. We don't want anyone wondering about us, especially if this other thing doesn't go away and the cops keep asking questions about her classmates."

"How would we show our patriotism?" one of the others asked.

"Well, for starters, I'm going to write to the newspaper and see if I can get Mr. Moore fired," Larry replied. Mr. Moore, Larry's civics teacher, had just led a class discussion on dissent in a free society. What did it mean to be patriotic in a democracy? Could you disagree with your government and march in the streets against its policies, seeking a more just society, and be considered as patriotic as the person who puts on a uniform and goes to war?

"I don't think so," Larry said.

Mr. Moore was young, in his late twenties, and a recent graduate of the University of Washington. Larry disagreed with Moore's thinking, but at the University of Washington, liberalism ran deep in the faculty.

Larry had learned something quite different from his dad – that patriotism meant you stood by your president and your flag no matter what, right or wrong.

Larry had heard his Navy dad talk about draft-dodgers and the anti-war movement, streets filled with drug addicts and kids who believed in free love, and losers opposed to U.S. victory in Vietnam. Lyndon Johnson was president, pushing a whole agenda of liberal programs through Congress, and the county was mired in the quagmire of Vietnam. Turncoats like Jane Fonda had gone to Hanoi, betrayed U.S. prisoners of war and given comfort to the enemy.

Marlene Meyers was sure to be elected student body president and she disdained those who disagreed with her views about politics and patriotism. Larry admired her intensely. She was the kind of leader the school needed – the nation.

"What are we going to call our group?" Dennis Delaney asked.

"How about The Brothers?" Larry replied.

One by one, the others agreed.

"What will The Brothers do?" one of the others asked.

"We'll watch until we see someone acting anti-Navy or anti-American, and then we'll take care of them quietly. That includes dirty tricks if we have to. You are all sworn to secrecy," and they all nodded.

"One thing I know for sure is that the newspapers in this community are on our side. The first thing I'm going to do is write a letter to the editor saying Mr. Moore is teaching Communist ideas in his classes. Then just sit back and watch what happens."

Ryan and Louise
1965

"Ladies and gentlemen," the principal spoke into his microphone from center court in the high school gym. "May I present your 1965 state wrestling champions, Ryan Ashford and Dennis Delaney!"

Students broke into applause and cheers, and stomped the bleachers with their feet. The high school band struck up, "Hey, Look Me Over." The two wrestlers loped out to center court in their purple-and-gold letter jackets, followed by the rest of the squad in a single-file line. The principal picked up a golden trophy from the table in front of him and handed it to Ashford, and then did the same with a second trophy for Delaney.

*

Hot breath fogged the windows of Ryan Ashford's two-door, nineteen-fifty-seven Chevrolet Bel Air. He was parked by the darkened high school football stadium in a prolonged embrace and kiss with Louise Kristoferson.

Kristoferson was a sophomore, two years behind Ashford. They had gone together throughout Ashford's senior year. He was a celebrity on campus now, having just won the state wrestling championship in his weight class. His parents had bought him the car as a reward for keeping his grades up and excelling in school sports. As used cars go, it was in mint condition with low miles.

Louise worked herself free of his kiss, shook her shoulder-length, black hair away from her eyes, and pushed Ryan back. "Ryan, I can't. What if I get pregnant? I want to make love to you but we can't go all the way right now."

"We'll get married when you graduate," Ashford said.

"I wish you weren't going into the Army."

"It's just a few years. By the time you finish school, I'll be a sergeant and we'll get a place of our own. Besides, my buddies and I are going to do our part to fight the liberals and Commies."

It was just like him to have a plan all mapped out like that for his life, Louise thought. He was always thinking ahead. For the last few years they had watched the United States sink deeper into the quagmire of Vietnam. For high school seniors like Ryan, it forced some soul-searching about their futures. He and Louise both knew that going to Vietnam was an early death sentence for some graduating seniors. The danger of war frightened Louise but appealed to the adventurer in Ryan.

The United States had fought to a costly and tense stalemate in Korea and the French had been driven out of Indochina. Russia had beaten the United States into space with the Sputnik satellite, a demoralizing blow to American pride. Communism had gained a foothold in the Western Hemisphere in Cuba, ninety miles from the U.S. mainland. The West was in retreat and Communism was gaining everywhere. Ryan was very serious about what was happening in the world. By contrast, Louise just wanted a good life, some babies and some romance.

As promised, Ryan came home on leave in July of 1967, right after Louise graduated, and they were married in a small Baptist church in Anacortes, in front of their parents and a few friends. Louise thought he was very handsome in his dress uniform and spit-shined shoes. Ryan's high school wrestling buddy, Dennis Delaney, was his best man. Ryan took Louise with him back to his duty station in Alabama, far from her family, and they got a small military duplex in family housing. But the excitement of their first home together soon faded for Louise. Ryan was gone all day to the post and she was home alone, time heavy on her hands.

The houses here all looked the same, spiritless, mirror images of each other, with cookie-cutter yards and on-street parking. Bicycles with training wheels lay on the ground wherever kids dropped them to do something else. Garbage in galvanized cans baked in the Southern sun, awaiting the Black men who came to take it away.

Louise hated the South's heat and humidity, and felt lost without the mountains and beaches of home. She and Ryan had passionate sex almost every day those first few months and Louise was surprised she didn't get pregnant. There was no life for her here.

More and more, her husband seemed consumed with race and politics, hippies, draft-dodgers, college students and anti-war protesters. He loved the plain-spoken George Wallace and his tough stance on segregation. Wallace was an old-style Southern political pro, walking the line between tough segregationist policies and repeated patronizing assurances that, "I love the Nigra and the Nigra loves me."

Ryan told Louise, "All our problems, all this unrest and agitation, started with Negroes in the military getting their so called 'equal rights' with the whites. They aren't equal and nothing's going to change that. Look at the way they live – like animals. I'll be damned if I'm going to take orders from a Negro."

FINAL COVER-UP

The French defeat in Vietnam had drawn the United States into Vietnam. "How could France let a bunch of gooks do that to them?" he asked. Louise had no answer. "Freedom is in retreat everywhere and no one has the backbone to do anything about it. Times like this call for us to stand up and be counted."

To Louise, it seemed like Ryan was drifting farther and farther from her. Instead of dreaming and building a future together, they were descending into separate worlds, with separate friends and priorities. Military housing and military wives were depressing.

When Ryan reenlisted, declaring his intention to make the military his career, she announced she wanted to move back to Anacortes and make their permanent home there, and find a job in an office. They would see each other when he came home on leave. He didn't object.

She found a one-bedroom cottage on Guemes Island, just across the channel from Anacortes, and watched the ferry cross back-and-forth all day. She found peace and contentment tending a few flowers and reading books, and making new friends, far from her husband and his angry ideology.

Louise had lost touch with most of her classmates, but still thought sometimes about Christy Morris. She'd liked her, and Louise never understood how someone could just disappear off the face of the earth. Someone must know something.

DAN PEDERSEN

Waiting

The two men talked just above a whisper as they waited in the darkness, in the woods, about a hundred feet down a rutted gravel driveway from a dilapidated old double-wide home. It was raining lightly, a week before Thanksgiving, 2008, and they were alert to any sounds.

It had been decades since high school and the unsolved disappearance of Christy Morris. They had both served several tours in the military and later as paramilitary contractors. Neither of them could add up all the people they'd killed. Now, the long tail of that first death in 1965 had come back to haunt them. Someone was holding it over them.

A single, dim porch light illuminated the clearing by the house, but at this distance they were beyond its reach. They used a small flashlight to keep from tripping over stumps and branches as they looked for a place to sit. A dense, November overcast blocked the moon. Droplets of water clung to the salal and huckleberry foliage. The smaller of the two men, wiry and intense, reached into his pocket for something. A brief flare lit both their faces as he scratched the flint of his cigarette lighter. A second later, with a clink, it was dark again.

"This is a shitty job," the smaller guy said. "We shouldn't be doing this."

"You're right. I don't like it any better than you

do," the other man said. "Larry says someone talked, and now if we don't do this, we've got prosecution hanging over us for that other business. Let's just do what we have to do to make everyone happy. I don't want to go back and answer questions about high school."

"There were only four of us who knew," the smoker said. "It shouldn't be that hard to find out who talked."

"I have my suspicions."

"Regardless of who it was, someone else knows now and they have the power to use it against us with the police. That's the bottom line."

"So, we don't even know who wants this guy killed tonight."

"That's how it looks. They know we know how to do it."

"And now they've got us over a barrel."

The two men fell silent. Finally, the taller man spoke. "Do you ever think about the girl?"

"Who? Christy?"

"Yeah. She'd have grandchildren now."

"I think about her, but don't remember the details very well. That night is a blur – like she never existed. I was pretty drunk. I just hear the thump. That's what stays with me – the thump."

"She was a nice kid," the taller man said.

"She was Colored. And I still don't understand what she was doing in the road. Those people ..."

"Maybe we should have handled things differently that night."

"Like what? We were drinking. Underage. I didn't have a license. My parents would have killed me," the smoker said.

"But yeah, we weren't thinking," he continued, tapping some ash off his cigarette. "Still, we did one thing right."

"What's that?"

"No one ever found the body."

The conversation went silent for another moment.

"Who is this guy, anyway?" the smoker asked. "Do you know anything about him?" Only the orange glow of his cigarette tip and a few puffs of white smoke revealed where he was sitting, on a fallen Hemlock.

"He's a lawyer," the taller man replied. "He's pushing a leftist agenda against Navy expansion, logging all over the island, downtown development and disturbing Indian graves on the waterfront. The higher ups are done trying to work with him. He's such an obstacle, he has to go."

The smoker went into a fit of coughing and cleared his throat. "He must be bad if somebody wants him dead."

"You should kick that habit," the second man said. "It's going to kill you.

"Where are you headed after tonight?" the smoker asked, tossing his cigarette on the ground and smashing it with his shoe till the glow died in a cloud of orange sparks.

"Back to Nicaragua," the taller man replied. "I've got some unfinished business there. You?"

"Middle East," Chesterfield Man confirmed. "I considered Central America but really hate snakes."

The taller man laughed. "I'd be more worried about an IED, if I were you."

The taller man gestured toward the modular home. "How can anyone live like that?" he asked. The porch light illuminated rust stains, blue tarps and stacks of firewood. "It's like the Ozarks." The yard was littered with old computers, a discarded TV, a refrigerator that had apparently broken down. The discards had made it no further than the yard.

The two men had gone over every step of the plan to leave no evidence, and had parked their stolen van out of sight in a nearby clearing.

As soon as they heard the old Toyota coming up

the narrow logging track to the house, they slipped black hoods over their heads and pulled Glock 45s from their coat pockets. The smoker stepped into the road, into the beam of the headlights, shielding his eyes against the blinding light and waving his arms for the pickup to stop. The taller man circled behind it where he could cover his partner and intercept the driver of the truck if he attempted to run.

The truck stopped and the driver unrolled his window and asked, "What is this? Halloween?"

The man holding the gun was confused. Who was the woman? There wasn't supposed to be any woman.

"We'd like you to come with us. Our boss would like to talk."

"He has a strange way of requesting a meeting. Maybe we should do our talking right here," the driver said.

"You don't understand. This is a polite request, but the alternative is impolite. Keep your hands where I can see them."

The couple in the truck opened their doors and got out. While one of the hooded men kept his gun on them, the other handcuffed them behind their backs and led them to the van hidden nearby, where he locked them in the windowless cargo bay. The other man, wearing rubber gloves, drove Langston's pickup the rest of the way to the cabin, parked it, opened the door to the mobile home and tossed the keys on the kitchen table.

Then he returned to the van, stopping for a moment with his penlight to find the Chesterfield butts and pocket them.

Marlene

"Oh, it does my heart good to see so many freedom-loving, red-blooded American patriots here this morning," Marlene shouted into her bullhorn as she paced back and forth on the courthouse steps. "You and I have a job to do, cleaning up the mess in county government. With your help I know we can do it."

"Mar-lene, Mar-lene, Mar-lene!" the crowd chanted.

Sheriff's Deputy Roger Gray watched with apprehension. Marlene Meyers was back after decades in Washington, D.C., where she'd been a Congressional aide and lobbyist for the oil and coal industries. After a successful first term as one of three county commissioners, now she was mounting an aggressive bid for reelection on a strident pro-Navy, pro-development platform, championing a large, proposed addition to the City of Oak Harbor that would bring 250 new homes. There were rumors the Navy was getting ready to station a noisy new electronic warfare jet on Whidbey Island, the EA-18G Growler, and Meyers would be all for it.

At sixty-one, she still had the striking good looks and dynamic speaking style that had propelled her to student body president in high school. Oak Harbor had been the scene of her earliest success in politics.

Now, buoyed by the emerging Tea Party Movement and the rise of Alaska Governor Sarah Palin as a national political figure, it looked to Roger like the charismatic Meyers was ready to make her move in island politics.

"We're going to kick start our local economy and jobs by getting those 250 homes built!" she declared. The crowd roared and waved their signs. "The 'anti's' have stood in the way too long. We're going to build those homes on my watch!

"And," she added, "we aren't going to let any long-dead Indians stop us from making Old Town the jewel of our commercial core.

"Liberals and socialists are running this county into the ground, killing jobs and stifling growth with their extreme environmental laws. They hate the Navy and hate our country. This has to stop, and I'm telling you it stops right now today. No more tyranny by the radical environmentalists!"

One of three county commissioners, Marlene had come up short of her challenger by 203 votes in her bid for reelection. She accused her colleagues and election officials of rigging the election.

A few concrete barricades and a cordon of county deputies, state patrol and National Guard troops stood between the demonstrators and the doors to the courthouse. The officers were lightly armed, mostly trading their firearms for nightsticks, body armor and face shields to avoid provoking a conflict. Roger hoped they weren't making a fatal mistake by underestimating what was unfolding here. My god, was Marlene going to get away with this?

Behind the demonstrators, a front loader with the words Trammel Excavating idled at the ready. Roger recognized Marvin Trammel at the controls. Nearby, Oak Harbor activist Larry Ward was talking with a small group of muscular, crewcut men. Toward the back of the group, Roger recognized developer Walter Gibbs, who seemed to be just watching. It made sense this would be a who's who of the development crowd. Their economic interests were paramount.

"Follow me!" Marlene shouted, and turned toward the courthouse. She walked a few steps and then drifted to the side, where several associates waited. Marvin Trammel gunned the engine of his front loader and advanced in a cloud of diesel, pushing aside the first barrier.

The crowd surged forward and started pushing and shoving the cordon of police.

"Back up and disperse," the police commander ordered the crowd. You are ordered to leave now."

One by one, demonstrators peeled away from the back of the crowd. Marlene and her entourage had disappeared.

Roger was taking pictures of as many demonstrators as he could. So was the newspaper. If prosecutions followed, the pictures would be critical. He was keeping an eye especially on Larry Ward, an outspoken right-wing activist from Oak Harbor known for his strident pro-Navy, anti-environment letters to the editor. Ward had a history of confrontation and had been in some minor physical skirmishes. There were rumors he was close to Marlene personally. Neither was married, and they were often seen together at political rallies and community events, and occasionally at restaurants.

"This was one of the strangest days in the history of Island County," the newspaper reported a couple of days later. "Commissioner Marlene Meyers made a desperate, last-ditch bid to reclaim her office by force. Meyers said she never intended her followers to engage in violence or destruction of property – she was just using the rhetoric of politics to motivate them.

"Police said Meyers did not participate directly in breaking any laws and will not be charged." Roger knew it was partly a political calculation by the sheriff to avoid further inflaming her followers.

FINAL COVER-UP

"It is rumored that Meyers is considering relocating to California and pursuing her political ambitions in the Golden State."

Dennis and Alicia

Dennis Delaney poked a stick at a few glowing coals in a firepit on the eastern shore of Lake Nicaragua. He was sitting with eight other figures, all wearing jungle fatigues, quietly eating from mess kits. They made no sounds but the occasional light clink of utensils on their aluminum kits, and a few whispers among them in Spanish.

The flickering light offered only glimpses of their faces, which were hidden partly by streaks of black grease paint to darken any reflections.

Seven of the figures were bearded; the eighth was not, and all sat within arm's reach of assault rifles and bandoliers laid out on the ground.

Delaney was talking with the eighth figure, a young nurse named Alicia they had extracted from a health clinic in one of the nearby villages. Her long black hair was tied tightly in a bun under her hat. This, plus the fatigues, minimized her femininity.

Delaney had not been with a woman in months and found her company refreshing. She was smart and obviously well bred, an intellectual, unlike these former government soldiers around the campfire. She had been working as an informant for them, providing information about troop movements by the Sandinista soldiers in this region. Dennis knew her story. Her parents and siblings had all been killed in a Sandinista raid a year ago. To survive, she had made a show of denouncing the government, but now Sandinista sympathizers in the village suspected her, she said, and would give her up to the soldiers the next time they came to the village.

"Chica," one of the fatigued men addressed her. "You like to party? Life is short."

She ignored the man. Delaney glared at him and turned back to Alicia.

"We can't take you with us," he said. "The way we live, the men ..." He left the thought unfinished.

"You must get me out of the country," she replied. "You have planes that land in the jungle. When the plane comes, put me on it. Make up some reason. Tell the pilot it's part of the mission – to ask no questions. I know the planes go back empty. Just get me to Florida and I'll disappear, and you'll never hear from me again."

"I can't."

"Yes, Dennis, you can. I know you can." She was using his first name now, peeling away the formalities that were the last wall between them.

"You have a mother, si? Maybe a sister? Imagine you could save their life."

It was an impossible request. The CIA did not rescue informants. If they had the bad luck to be caught, he was sorry but it was just the nature of this awful conflict. All wars have casualties. People were dying on both sides for no good reason, as if they had never lived. He was here as an instrument of U.S. policy, not a savior to the indigenous population.

In a few days, a month, it would make no difference whether this young Alicia had helped them or not. She would just be so many dusty bones in a shallow grave in the jungle somewhere.

On the other hand, she had a spirit, a quality, that touched him. She was a fighter, a survivor, and was fighting for her life right now with him.

"Tell me about yourself, Dennis," she said. "Did

you grow up in a nice place? Not like here, I'm sure."

"I grew up on an island, very beautiful," he replied. "But I can't talk about it. My job ..."

Under different circumstances, he could imagine sitting down with her at a sidewalk café, she in a white sundress and dark glasses, smiling like they shared some special secret, and having a lively discussion of art and politics over their coffees.

It would have to be in a different lifetime.

Delaney's mission tonight as the leader of this small band was to enter a local village, kidnap the pro-Sandinista mayor, and take him to the church, where the Nicaraguans would question and execute him along with the priest. The village was known to be sympathetic to Cuban leader Fidel Castro. Government troops had been here two days earlier and moved on.

Delaney had followed the Sandinista revolution since shortly after graduation from high school. He'd served one term in the Army, become a contractor and then been recruited by the CIA, partly because he spoke Spanish. Leftist university students, youth leaders and priests had organized the movement against Nicaraguan President Anastasio Somoza, who was massively corrupt but steadfastly pro-American. As long as he held power, the rebels would have a hard time spreading Communist influence in Central America.

The CIA had waged a shadow war against the Sandinistas since they overthrew Somoza in 1979. In 1981, President Ronald Reagan had signed a secret document authorizing the CIA to create a five-hundred-man force of Nicaraguan Contras to undermine Sandinista control of the country. Reagan was convinced they were supplying large volumes of weapons to rebel groups in El Salvador, and that the Sandinistas were proxies of the Soviet Union.

It felt good to be fighting Communism on the front lines, but it could be confusing at times. Some of the Contra soldiers seemed to enjoy interrogations for the sheer pleasure, and some of their victims were clearly innocent. The Sandinistas had carried out atrocities against the civilian population, but had also introduced reforms including a mass literacy push, gender equality reforms and greater access to healthcare. In this conflict nothing was clear.

In high school, when he and his wrestling-squad buddies had pledged themselves to direct action, the sides in the Cold War had seemed clearer. America needed heroes. It was under attack from both outside and within. Delaney, Ashford, Ward and Trammel had gone different directions after graduation but remained true to their pledge and to one another. Life was a clear choice between good and evil. All four understood this.

But that didn't help him with Alicia. What to do about her?

Forensics

"Kat, it's Ralph Emerson," the voice on the telephone began.

Kat had been awaiting a report from Dr. Emerson, the county coroner, on the bones discovered in the sinkhole in Old Town. With his white hair and soft-spoken manner, the doctor reminded Kat of the devoted and beloved Jim Anderson in old episodes of *Father Knows Best.*

"The taller individual – six foot four, was Elliott Langston, as you expected," Dr. Emerson said. "We matched his dental work with files from his dentist in Coupeville."

"Cause of death?" Kat asked.

"Gunshot to the back of the head, execution style."

"Any other injuries?"

"No broken bones. Nothing to indicate any trauma other than what you'd expect being from being dumped in a hole and covered with rocks and gravel."

"What about the other skeleton?"

"Female, about five-foot-eight," based on the pelvis and femurs. I'd say she was about thirty-five and had never had children. No history of broken bones. Very little dental work – she had good teeth."

"Cause of death?" Kat asked.

"The same. Gunshot to the back of the head."

So, it was now clear that Elliott Langston had been murdered around the time of his disappearance, in November of 2008, and his remains buried under the street at that time while it was dug up for repair. But who was the woman? She did not fit any known disappearances from that time on the island. How did she come to be executed and buried in the same hole as a bachelor environmentalist who lived in a dilapidated trailer in the woods?

"Can you run DNA analysis on the woman's bones?" Kat asked.

"We certainly can. I'm moving ahead with that now."

The circumstances of the two murders troubled Kat. They were not a crime of passion or the work of someone who was thinking on the fly as he went. It appeared every step had been well planned. When Detective Shane Lindstrom returned to the Freeland precinct office that afternoon, Kat was waiting and took him aside to discuss the case. Shane sat down and leaned back in his chair as Kat found a spot to prop herself on the corner of his desk.

"These were professional hits," Kat said. "Not only did the killer leave no evidence, no trail, but he was absolutely cold-blooded about it. If you were looking for such a person in Island County, where would you look?"

Shane thought a moment. "It could be a hardcore ex-con, someone who had murdered before. Or the trigger man may have been an outsider brought in by someone to do the job. We have a large military community here, too. It's possible it was the work of a special forces soldier, or perhaps a private contractor who served in the Middle East and learned how to kill."

"So, if it was a soldier, whomever hired this person," Kat began, "would have needed connections in the military community. They needed to know someone, or someone who knew someone, they could approach to hire it done. They needed a place to carry out the murders where they wouldn't be observed and could clean up the evidence. And then they needed a place to dump the bodies. Given where the bodies had been found, they needed a gravel truck, most likely."

"A gravel truck seems like the logical way to transport the bodies," Shane said, "but we should keep an open mind that the killer could have delivered the bodies some other way, or had the help of accomplices working on the street repair."

"You knew Elliott Langston."

"A little. Just from watching him at hearings and reading about him in the newspaper."

"Was he a ladies' man?"

"I would say no. I never heard of him being with a woman. He was quite a geek, physically odd, to be blunt. I have trouble picturing him bringing home a woman for a one-night stand, if that's what you're asking. But, you know," he said hesitatingly, "people can surprise you."

Walter Gibbs

Lawyer's Remains Found Under Old Town Street

"The 2008 disappearance of Coupeville environmental lawyer Elliott Langston is now being investigated as part of a double murder," began the page one story in the island newspaper. *Langston's skeletal remains were found last week during a street repair in Oak Harbor's Old Town and detectives have positively identified them from dental records.*

But now they now face a new mystery: Who was the woman executed and buried alongside him when the street was dug up in 2008? And why did someone want either of them dead?

One of the keys to this case was finding out who had access to the street project worksite. Someone had been able to deposit the two bodies in the hole undetected.

A visit to the city's public works department identified Walter Gibbs as the general contractor, supported by half-a-dozen subs. Kat called ahead and requested a meeting with him.

Kat found Gibbs's office on the upper level of a two-story commercial building on Oak Harbor's Midway Boulevard. There wasn't much doubt because just one vehicle was parked on the street in front of it, a white Cadillac Escalade with gold trim and personalized plates: "Gibbs."

When the receptionist led Kat into Gibbs's office, her eye landed right away on a large, aerial photograph behind his desk of what was obviously a planned community of houses and streets. There must have been at least a hundred houses in the picture, and it was labeled on the frame, "Gibbs Addition."

Gibbs stood and extended his hand, which caused his cufflinked sleeves to ride up and reveal a magnetic, copper arthritis bracelet on his left wrist. Apparently, he liked shiny things because he was wearing a gold chain under his open-collar shirt. He had a warm smile and gentle eyes, and was much larger than she expected, somewhere north of 250 pounds. He appeared to be a man of big appetites and one look told her he liked to laugh.

"I must say," she began, "you have an unusual name. I'm not sure I've run into it before."

"What? Walter?" he joked, and slapped his knee as he bent forward laughing. "I'm North Carolinian and one of just a few Gibbs in my county. The origin is Scottish and, I understand, ranks 498th in popularity among American surnames, since you brought it up."

"Are there any others around here?" Kat asked.

"I don't think so. My parents are both deceased. They had just two children, and my sister in California passed away some years ago."

"I'm sorry," Kat said. "How did she die?"

"We don't know," Gibbs said. "She disappeared from her home and was never seen again. I looked for her, and so did the police. She just vanished."

He added, "I miss her every day."

His eyes were misting and Kat gave him a moment to compose himself, then asked, "What can you tell me about the Old Town street project of 2008?"

"You mean Elliott Langston's final resting place, the sinkhole of 2019?" he replied. He gestured at the front page of the newspaper on his desk. "That's been a trouble spot for years. The old infrastructure in the street keeps breaking down."

"You were the general contractor back in 2008," Kat said. "Can you remember any suspicious activity involving access to the worksite?"

"Not really. We kept it pretty well secured for obvious liability reasons."

"Including nighttime?"

"We had it cordoned off, with barriers and flashing lights. No one expects someone to mess with a hole on the ground at night, nor can you really prepare for something like that."

"But," Kat said, "we now know it became the final resting place of Elliott Langston and an unidentified woman. Someone was able to dump their bodies into the hole and cover them with enough gravel that they were never found until now. Can you give me the names of the people who were hauling gravel and operating machinery at that time?"

"Of course," Gibbs said. "I can do it off the top of my head, but I'll also vouch that they were good companies – nothing shady or questionable about them." He rattled off the names of the companies that hauled gravel and installed the new drainage culvert. Kat's ears perked up when he mentioned Trammel Excavating. She made a mental note to come back to Trammel later.

"I couldn't help noticing the photograph behind you, Gibbs Addition," Kat said.

"Yes, that's one of ours – our biggest project. It was years in the planning and permitting, but, by golly, we got 'er done."

"I can't imagine the patience it takes to carry out such a complex process," Kat remarked.

Gibbs smiled, pleased it appeared that someone

appreciated how hard his job was as a developer. Kat was good at this, setting a subject at ease with a sense that she sympathized with his perspective.

"Just acquiring the land at reasonable prices was a big part of it," Gibbs said. "Prices go up the second someone gets wind of what you might be thinking, so we used third-party companies to buy various parcels, so the pattern of ownership wouldn't be obvious. And then there's all the city requirements, the endless permit process, and of course the legal and court battles to go ahead with development ..." Gibbs's voice trailed off. "I'm proud of it – a huge benefit to the tax base of Oak Harbor. People were just sitting on that land, getting no benefit from it. We put cash in their pockets. We took some junky forest and farmland and turned them into acres of lawns and streets, and playgrounds for the kids."

"Was Elliott Langston a part of those legal battles?" Kat asked.

"Of course, he was part of everything that happened or didn't happen in this county. You had to respect the guy – a worthy adversary. But I guess a backwoods North Carolinian is a pretty stubborn adversary, too." Gibbs laughed and Kat smiled noncommittally.

FINAL COVER-UP

The Woman
November 2008

The young woman sat alone, just behind and across from the driver, as the Island Transit bus cruised north on Highway 20. In her thirties, she was wearing blue jeans and a black sweatshirt, and a white baseball cap, with her ponytail tucked through the gap in the back. She was the only passenger on this leg of the trip to Coupeville, having boarded at the Clinton ferry landing with several teenagers who had gotten off in Freeland and an elderly couple who had gone as far as Greenbank. The sun had set hours ago on this November evening. It was raining lightly and she hoped the man she was meeting would be waiting as promised.

"How far are you going tonight?" the driver asked, glancing over at her. "Don't think I've seen you on my bus before."

"Coupeville," she said. "I'm just off the plane from California. I have a brother in Oak Harbor but don't know if I'll see him on this trip."

"It'd be a shame to miss the opportunity. You'll like Coupeville. It's quiet but picturesque. We've got some good restaurants and a great bookstore, if you like books."

"I do. Hey, do you know anything about Native

American settlements around Coupeville? I'm interested in the Native history of this place."

The driver nodded. "The story is that there were settlements and longhouses all around Penn Cove. There's an old shell midden at Monroe Landing that goes back four thousand years, where they dumped their baskets of garbage. Can you imagine that? Whites have lived here about one hundred fifty years, but before that the Skagits were here for thousands of years."

The woman pictured generations of Native women dumping baskets of shells, fish carcasses, duck bones and other kitchen garbage in a mound by the beach, along with broken children's toys and other debris from the settlement. Hundreds of years later, layers of sediment in these garbage dumps often stood out as nutrient-rich black bands in the shoreline bluffs. Almost all the shells were upside down, the result of baskets being turned upside down to dump their contents. Over time, the nutrient-rich soil in these areas grew lush weeds and grasses that stood out prominently from the surrounding shoreline.

"It's hard to believe such a long civilization ended so abruptly just a century and a half ago," the woman said.

"Well," the driver said, "all they had were canoes. We've got buses and jet airplanes," and he laughed.

They drove on in silence for a few minutes.

"Is someone meeting you in Coupeville?" the driver asked. "It can be a lonely place after dark."

"A friend, I think. I hope," she said.

Elliott Langston had sounded pleasant and genuine on the phone. She already knew he was smart – a very sharp lawyer. She felt she was a good judge of people and hoped she was right about him as well. She'd gotten to know him in several calls over the past month, in which she had given him details of shady land transactions on the island.

They had also spoken of the interest they both shared in the island's native history. She knew that the Skagit peoples occupied the northern and central parts of the island, and the Snohomish the south, around Langley and Sandy Point. The local bands lived peaceably and intermarried, but had to be alert to slave-raiding parties of northern Indians who sometimes ventured south into these waters.

The woman wasn't looking for a romantic encounter and it seemed neither was he – they were both simply doing what they thought was right. He had offered her a place to stay in his modular home – "nothing fancy, but a clean room" – and she had accepted on faith.

The woman had flown from Fresno to Seattle and taken an airport van to Mukilteo, where she caught the boat to the island.

"That's the Prairie Station Transit Park just ahead," the driver alerted her, "and maybe that's your friend waiting for you."

The woman peered through the windshield and saw a man who looked like Jesus standing next to an old Toyota pickup. That would be Elliott.

The bus pulled to a stop and the driver lowered the front end to a kneel with a hiss so she could disembark with fewer steps. She grabbed a backpack from the seat beside her and moved to the top of the stairs.

"Have a good evening," the driver called to her as he swung the door shut and hit the button to raise the front of the bus again.

"Patty, welcome," Elliott greeted her. "I'm glad to see you."

"Likewise," she said. "I feel like we're old friends."

"Well, sometimes I just feel old," Elliott said. "It's been a long week of fighting battles. I'm looking forward to a few days of talking with you and learning what you know about how your brother acquired so much land."

"Is it far to your home?" she asked.

"Not far at all. Let's get you settled. Have you had dinner? Tomorrow we'll run up to Oak Harbor and look around Old Town and Maylor's Point, where the Skagits buried many of their dead. And I'll show you some areas being logged and developed. Then you'll really understand the importance of what you're doing here."

"I'd like to see whatever you can show me of the Native history, too," the woman said.

"Not much is visible anymore, but the county museum is a good place to start."

It was just fifteen minutes till they turned onto a gravel driveway in the woods. The Toyota bounced as Elliott negotiated ruts and holes in the road. The woman was shocked when the headlights finally swept across the old modular home, but surprised even more when a man in a black hood, holding a gun, stepped in front of the truck and waved it to a stop.

"What's this?" the woman asked.

"I don't know. Nothing good."

The Quarry

The men drove north through the night on Highway 20, meeting just a few oncoming cars. It was raining now, windshield wipers slapping at the downpour pelting the vehicle. It was a miserable night.

A few miles north of Oak Harbor, they turned onto a little-used gravel road, released a padlock that held a chain across the road, and proceeded into a clearing. The van emerged into an earthen amphitheatre, its headlights sweeping across piles of dirt and gravel, rusty old machinery and ancient gas cans and oil barrels, and large puddles of rainwater.

They stopped, shut off the engine, got out and pulled their guns from their shoulder holsters. With the taller man standing back, the wiry man opened the rear doors of the van.

"This is your stop," he said to the prisoners, gesturing with his pistol for the two to get out. He reached into his pocket and retrieved a silencer, and screwed it onto the barrel of his gun.

He could see Elliott's eyes darting between him and the other man. It was the typical last look he'd seen many times on the faces of young Arabs. *Allahu Akbar!* they would all shout when there was nothing left to say. Elliott would try to negotiate now.

"Let's talk about this," Elliott said. "We can work something out, and whatever's the problem, she's totally innocent."

"Not going to happen," the armed man said.

"Where's The Boss? You said someone wanted to talk."

"Couldn't make it tonight. Turn around and get down on your knees, please. Let's not make this any messier for you than it needs to be."

Langston hesitated, as if weighing his options in this hopeless situation. Finally, he turned and got down. The man fired point blank into the back of Langston's head and then did the same with the woman. Blood exploded from their throats and merged into the soupy mess of rainwater on the ground. This rain was doing them a favor.

Then, the two men removed all I.D. and personal effects, undressed the two victims and dragged them to a spot in some low brush at the edge of the clearing.

"Who's the woman?" the wiry man asked.

The taller man flipped open her wallet. "Someone with a California driver's license. Wrong place, wrong time."

They piled the victims' clothes and identification into the front seat of the van, soaked the interior thoroughly with ten gallons of gasoline from cans stashed nearby, and tossed a match at it. With a whoosh, flames erupted everywhere and shot thirty feet into the air.

A tongue of fire came toward the man holding the can. He dropped it and reeled back from the blinding flash and heat. The fire was concealed from passersby on the highway by the bowl of trees and terrain surrounding the site, and there were no Navy jets flying tonight. The fire raged for twenty minutes and kept the men warm before it subsided to a few lingering wisps of smoke. It stank of petroleum and plastic upholstery and wiring. Rain continued to fall and the hot metal steamed itself.

The men peered into the front seat and all they

saw was ash. The seat was just springs where they'd piled the clothes and I.D. They patted the ground and pocketed their two shell casings. They had already scratched out the vehicle identification number of the stolen van and removed its license plates. It would soon be just another rusting hulk in this forgotten place.

The shooter, the smaller, bald-headed guy, smoked a Chesterfield and mashed the butt with his boot. Then he pulled out his cell phone, dialed a number and spoke three words: "All done here."

After a few moments, thoroughly soaked, they were on their separate ways on motorbikes previously stationed at the gravel pit.

*

Marvin Trammel awoke to the buzzing vibration of his cell phone. Confused, he groped for it on the table by his bedside and found it. Groggy and barely coherent, he answered in a low voice, trying not to awaken his wife: "Trammel."

"Marvin," the voice on the telephone began. "I need you to take your loader right now and pick up twelve yards of fill at the old quarry."

"Do you know what time it is?" he whispered.

The caller ignored him. "There are some remains in the brush that need to go on the load and you'll see what they are. Take the whole works to the Old Town dig tonight and dump it in the hole. Don't ask any questions. Don't wonder about anything. You're just delivering fill. I'll tell the site supervisor there's a load incoming overnight and you're handling it personally, and he doesn't need to be there."

He was wide awake now. Was this really happening? He was getting pulled into something. People with big machines and connections knew about shortcuts.

Trammel arrived at the quarry at one a.m. and laid out the ramps for his front loader. It was raining and he was going to get soaked. With the bright lights of the machine and his gleaming gravel truck, he could see the clearing well. His eye went right to two objects in the brush at the edge – human bodies, naked.

Oh god, he thought. Two? Nobody said anything about a woman? Why me? He stepped closer and saw they were lying face up -- Elliott Langston and some woman. He felt a rumble in his gut, doubled over and threw up. Dear god, what was this?

He wanted no part of this, but someone was holding Christy Morris over him. He got back on his machine and scooped two big buckets of gravel into his truck, so the bodies would not end up on the top of the hole when he dumped his load. Then he backed up, pushed the throttle straight ahead and neatly lifted the bodies into the air and onto the half-filled load. At least he didn't have to touch them with his hands.

He continued to dig gravel until the truck was full, and fastened a tarp over it to comply with state regulations. The bodies were now under tons of rock, the skin torn, tightly crushed and compressed, and likely unrecognizable from the weight. The last thing he needed was for anyone to stop him tonight and look at his load.

He drove home, disconnected the lowboy with the front loader from the back of his truck, and got to the dump site in Oak Harbor at 3:11 a.m. By 3:30 he had tipped the load into the hole, rolled up the tarp and reclosed the barriers blocking access to the site. With a flashlight from the cab, he scanned every inch of the hole and could see nothing but gravel. Elliott and his companion were somewhere underneath all that, gone from the face of the Earth.

At 4 a.m. he returned to bed. His wife, stirring only slightly, said nothing, rolled over and fell back to sleep. She always said she was a good sleeper. Trammel was not. He lay awake until 5 a.m., when he got up and brewed coffee. He piled his muddy, rain-soaked clothes into the washing machine and hit "start." By 7 a.m., he had finished and was folding the wash.

"Marvin, you did laundry in the middle of the night?" his wife asked as she walked into the kitchen. "What got into you?"

"I couldn't sleep," he said. "Needed something to do."

Ma Barker

Kat stood by the roadside, looking out across forty acres of slash and debris. In the distance, a white pickup truck with a diesel tank in its bed was parked in a clearing by several large, orange machines that were cutting and stacking logs. The heart of the operation, she knew from talking with long-time woodsmen, was the feller-buncher, a machine that can wrap its arms around a tree and cut it in the upright position before felling it, enabling loggers to clear acres of land within days that might have taken weeks or months of heavy labor by men with chainsaws and wedges before.

She and her husband, Guy, had talked about forest processes in connection with his work as a marine biologist for the county. They had both grown up close to nature – she as a runaway living in the wilds of the Adirondacks, and he as a Shoshone from southern Idaho, whose people felt a strong connection to wildlife and the Earth.

Until this week, this tract of forest had been home to hundreds of squirrels and chipmunks, raccoons, deer, coyotes, woodpeckers and a myriad of other wildlife species whose nests and territories had been disrupted.

They would find new ranges or territories, the

coyotes no doubt expanding onto neighboring properties and establishing new dens. Adversity just made them stronger and more adaptive to humans. They would show up in homeowners' back yards, visiting chicken coops, and watching and learning the routines of small dogs and cats. Every so often, a favorite pet would disappear without a trace. The squeeze against habitat and wildlife was never-ending. The coyotes became more urban all the time.

The tree canopy and a deep bed of fallen needles on the ground dampened and absorbed rainwater, so that nothing ran off.

Now, in the wake of the logging, large areas of the earth were compacted, and Kat could see water standing in broad pools from recent rains, with nowhere to go.

She unclipped a chain that was blocking the access road to the back of the property and proceeded slowly toward the group of vehicles, her red-and-blue flashers giving them plenty of warning of her approach.

Ahead, she saw the door of the pickup open and a stocky, short brunette in overalls get out, holding a walkie talkie in her left hand.

Kat pulled to a stop and opened her door.

"Are you Ma Barker?" she asked.

"You bet," the woman replied. "Is there some problem? Somebody trying to shut me down?"

"No, I just wanted to ask what you remember about 2008," Kat said.

"I was younger and prettier, and had a figure and a husband. Is that why you drove all the way out here?"

Kat smiled. She had been reluctant to address Kate Barker as "Ma," mindful of the violent reputation of the 1930s criminal matriarch. But loggers assured her it was the only name Kate used. She had adopted it after her husband's death in a logging accident and seemed proud of it, because no one could mow down trees as fast as she could.

In the logging business, it was necessary to work fast. Opposition usually formed within days after neighbors realized that a large tract of nearby forest was being cleared. If a logger worked fast enough, he could have all the trees on the ground before anyone even had time to lodge a complaint. Then all that remained was an ugly scar that took years to heal.

Elliott Langston was wise to this tactic and good at reacting fast. He had a close circle of informants who kept an eye out for equipment being moved, and tipped him of any sign that logging might be imminent on a parcel of land.

The newspaper article asking for the public's help in the 2008 case had brought a handful of tips, including an anonymous phone message to the effect. "Talk to Ma Barker. She knows something about it."

Kat gathered her thoughts. "You knew Elliott Langston, I take it."

"Asshole."

"I'm looking for people who can help me reconstruct what he was working on in 2008, who might have wished him gone, and who might know something about the woman whose body was found next to his in Old Town."

"Who wanted him gone? Me."

"What was the problem?"

"The usual. I had just started a big clearcut next to the prairie in Coupeville when he showed up with old wetland maps and tied the whole thing up with the county. He was on it so fast I barely got the bulldozer off the truck."

"Do you know anything about the woman whose remains were found with him?" Kat asked.

"Not really. Back around that time, there were rumors he was being fed information from out of state about some of the operations he was trying to stop. I don't know who that would have been. Out-of-state interests are behind a lot of the logging on the island."

"Including some of your jobs?"

"Yeah. Of course. They pay the bills. Unfortunately, the out-of-staters give a bad reputation to those of us who live here, with their lowball offers."

Kat couldn't help thinking about the Salish, who lived in peace and balance with nature for generations on the shores of Oak Harbor Bay and Penn Cove. *We sure screwed it up,* she thought, *for a little short-sighted gain.*

Right now, she needed to talk with Roger and Shane some more, and she knew just where she wanted to do that. It would take her a couple of hours to get ready and make the phone calls.

Double Bluff

Kat looked across the water at the Seattle skyline and the snowy profile of Mount Rainier on the horizon. This was her favorite hour at Double Bluff Beach on a hot summer day, toward dinnertime when the crowds had mostly dispersed home and the sun was lower in the sky. The early-evening sun felt good on her face, warming her cheeks and forehead around the rims of her stylish, round sunglasses.

"Those aren't your usual military-style gold-rims, said Roger Gray, the white-bearded, retired deputy sitting next to her on a large drift log. He had worked the Elliott Langston disappearance in 2008.

"No, they're my kick-back sunglasses, in which I channel the spirit of my friend, Marie Martin." Marie was the federal wildlife agent who had turned Kat's life around when she tackled her outside a family vacation lodge in the Adirondack Mountains where she'd been cabin-prowling a few years earlier.

"I think I'm ready for one of those brownies," Gray said.

"Make that two," added Kat's partner and mentor, Shane Lindstrom. Having a dinner picnic here this evening was Kat's idea, to clear her mind and get a fresh perspective on the case. Shane and Roger were the two colleagues she respected more than any others in the department. In fact, Shane was the whole reason she had landed this job she loved, and a new life that gave her a sense of purpose and fulfillment.

Roger's black lab, *Midnight,* sat directly in front of Kat, watching every morsel that passed from her plate to her mouth. Every so often, *Midnight's* tongue licked his lips. His eyes never left her.

"He isn't going to sing, is he?" Kat asked. "That would break my heart."

"That's up to you," Roger said. "I don't know how much more of this torture he can take."

Kat reached into her picnic basket and found a boneless chicken thigh, and delivered it to *Midnight's* mouth. He took the prize gently, careful not to rake any teeth across Kat's hand. He wagged and trotted away.

"I feel like we're missing something," she said as she passed around the tin of brownies. Roger chose a big corner piece and dropped a few crumbs down the front of his shirt. "I'm retired," he explained.

"What else was going on in 2008 that might have been behind the murders?" she asked.

Shane thought a moment. "There was that whole Marlene Meyers thing. But offhand I don't know how it fits."

"That's right," Roger said. "What a screwy time that was in Island County."

Meyers had been elected one of three county commissioners, from the populist Meyers Party, Roger said. "Her colleagues on the commission were a liberal Democrat and a swing Republican who tended to vote with her more often than against. Meyers had quite a movement behind her, self-appointed patriots, gun lovers and conspiracy theorists who fancied themselves starting a grassroots revolution to overturn county, state and federal government."

"Things got pretty intense," Shane added. "Meyers was so vulgar and divisive that she polarized the whole island. I don't know how she did it but she 'packaged' herself for evangelicals as a big champion of religious freedom. We had protesters in front of the courthouse with guns. People broke into county offices, or tried to. Some of the sheriff's deputies sided with the protesters and others sided against them. The Navy got involved. It's a multi-racial organization, of course, and racism doesn't set well. It was a mess."

Gray added, "It reached a crescendo when she lost an election to a liberal Democrat and refused to concede, claiming the vote was rigged, manipulated by the liberal Deep State. Thousands of her followers went along with every word of it."

"How come I never heard about this?" Kat asked.

"It was before your time. It fizzled out after a few years, but kinda came roaring back more recently with the dark turn in Presidential politics."

"I still don't see a connection to Elliott Langston," Kat said.

"Marlene was militantly pro-development, racist and anti-minority," Shane said. "That whole business of an Indian burial ground in Oak Harbor just galled her no end. She said we were letting a bunch of primitive, dead savages stand in the way of progress and economic development. Langston was livid because, among other things, he had a great interest in the early Salish history of the island and how the natives had lived so harmoniously with the land."

Kat had not been aware of Langston's strong feelings about the sacred burial ground of Oak Harbor. Maybe she'd been on the wrong track, thinking his murder had been over environmental conflicts. Maybe he had clashed with Meyers in a way that threatened her perception of economic development and she'd had her fill of him. Burying an Indian-lover under the street in the old Native burial ground would be a fitting, symbolic way to dispense with his remains. If so, maybe the woman who was found with him had something to do with that.

"How much do you know about the history of this conflict in Oak Harbor?" Kat asked Shane.

"The city is struggling to define itself and its heritage. In the early years of white settlement, it was a sleepy agricultural community that shipped crops and lumber by sea to the outside world. There were several piers for ships. Travel off island was by canoe originally, and later small steamships."

"It sounds pleasant," Kat said.

"Everything changed in a heartbeat after Deception Pass Bridge was built in the Depression years, opening a highway link for development. Then it changed exponentially around World War II when the Navy built its base at Oak Harbor, bringing a huge expansion of population, mostly young transient people with no particular ties to the community."

"And this means ...?"

"With the explosive population growth there were huge environmental losses – increased water pollution and depletion of salmon and marine life in Oak Harbor Bay, for example."

"I suppose that's inevitable," Kat said.

"It doesn't have to be, but to avoid it, you have make protecting the marine environment a priority, and in those days it wasn't. There was this feeling that the ocean was inexhaustible and could absorb anything we did to it."

Shane added, "Probably the worst part was surface-water runoff carrying hydrocarbons from vehicles, asbestos from brakes, that sort of thing. In the 1930s there were dozens of salmon fishing resorts around Puget Sound where you could rent a kicker boat for a dollar and catch a forty-pound fish. Today the fish and the resorts are gone – you're lucky to catch a four-pounder. The native heritage and original character of the shoreline were rapidly lost."

"So can Oak Harbor ever again be what it once was?" Kat asked.

"That would be asking a lot, but in recent years, there's been a push to reverse some of that damage, build shoreline trails and buffer areas, bring back nature, replant Garry Oaks and engage in interpretive education to honor Salish history and the original character of the land. The town is looking for an identity beyond the military. They'd like to have some of the tourist charm of Coupeville and Langley. Of course, not everyone thinks that's worth doing. They'd be happy if the whole island just turned into Federal Way."

"Where is Marlene now?" Kat asked.

Roger looked up. "Last I heard, Southern California. She ran for state legislature and lost, thank goodness. Last I knew, she was running a jobs program for veterans.

"Does she still have financial interests in Oak Harbor?"

"Oh, you bet she does," Shane said. "She's got her fingers in all kinds of housing and development projects here that serve the Navy. With the big expansion of the Growler jet training program on the island, the base is big business."

All this time Kat had assumed Langston's murder was the work of one individual with a specific grievance. Now for the first time she was beginning to wonder if more than one had gotten together on it for more than one reason, and just how high up the crime went.

Kat looked around. High on the bluff, a puff of dust rose into the air as a small slide tumbled down its steep face. Guy called this place an active feeder bluff, and it was actively eroding right in front of her. Sand from the bluff fell to the beach and was distributed by shoreline currents, forming a broad, sandy beach where there would otherwise be rocky cobble. The fine material created an ideal medium for eelgrass and the forage fish that formed the base of the food chain for salmon and orcas. Kat had learned that much from Guy. She loved knowing how things worked.

Kat needed to find out a lot more about Marlene Meyers, but right now she also needed to take care of a small personal matter that could cause some ripples at home.

Duncan

"Roger Gray sent me," Kat said to the woman at the motel's front desk.

"You're the deputy who's interested in *Duncan*," the woman confirmed. Kat nodded. "I've got him segregated so no one else will come along and adopt him before you have a chance to meet him."

She led Kat into the lunchroom in back. One look at the white spots on the black nose and front paws, and Kat was in love. *Duncan's* tail was already thumping. With his lush, long, black coat, he had the look of a classic herder, but his legs were short. The woman called him a Border Corgi. She opened the gate of the cage. Kat had come equipped with some small pieces of dried bacon in her pocket and *Duncan* eased forward tentatively. He was just the right size – not a rug rat and not a big, fearsome brute. Kat could see intelligence in his eyes.

She could feel him shaking.

"He's a little frightened," the woman said. "He's been through a lot."

Roger, with all his contacts in the dog world, had learned of *Duncan* just yesterday. "You'll have to act fast if you're interested," he said. "Several people already have their eye on him."

Duncan had arrived on the island from a kill shelter in Moses Lake, where he was scheduled to be euthanized. The shelter on the other side of the mountains was the last stop for strays and problem dogs picked up from local farms, or running feral in the rural countryside. They held onto strays for a few days to see if anyone claimed them, but the volume of incoming dogs meant they had to put down those that were unclaimed to make room for more.

The local shelter had a policy of not accepting dogs from off island, but some of the local dog lovers kept in touch with the manager in Moses Lake about dogs that might be especially adoptable. They had singled out *Duncan* and brought him, off the books, to the west side, hoping to find a good home for him by word of mouth.

"We don't know anything about his history," the motel manager said. "Sometimes these farm dogs have to live outdoors by their wits. They don't get a lot of love and can come with baggage that takes years to solve. Is your husband on board with this?"

"Oh absolutely, one hundred percent," Kat lied. "He's been after me to find us a dog." She knew *Duncan* was going to be a magnificent distraction and hoped he wouldn't interfere with her work. She'd let him ride along in the car sometimes if the sheriff didn't object. She had a secret plan for training him. Roger's lab, *Midnight*, would be *Duncan's* teacher dog, modeling confident, calm, mature behavior.

"Then let's get him packed up and get you on your way."

*

"You did *what?*" Guy demanded. "You know we talked about this and now isn't a good time. We're both so consumed with our careers."

"I know you said no, but a chance like this doesn't come along every day. He's perfect for me and I really need a dog to help me lighten up and decompress from my work."

Duncan was sitting in a heap just inside the kitchen door while the argument unfolded, not moving a muscle.

"Have you ever trained a dog?" Guy asked? "No. Do you know what kind of work it is? Not a clue. Are you prepared to give him the time and exercise he needs? No."

"Yes," Kat objected. "He's going to be my running partner and probably ride shotgun with me in the cruiser."

"That's ridiculous and you know it. You can't take the family dog on sheriff's business."

"Lower your voice," Kat said. "Dogs are sensitive and he's picking up the stress in this room. Give him a chance and you're going to love this guy." The dog's big, brown eyes were locked on Kat, his eyebrows arching and deflating as she made the case for him.

"Three days," Guy said. "He can stay here three days, and if it isn't working out, you'll have to take him back."

Penn Cove

Walter Gibbs sipped his first cup of coffee and looked out across the rolling fields north of Penn Cove. The scene was a patchwork of well-spaced farmhouses and fields, the landscape meandering gently down toward the blue waters of Penn Cove. Across the way, he could make out the village of Coupeville, and, to the east, the north end of Camano Island. The sun was just rising over the Cascade Mountains. This would be a beautiful day.

He and Judy had chosen this spot on Zylstra Road, south of Oak Harbor, for its pastoral character. It reminded Walter of home and his childhood. He felt a part of the land here. For Judy, it was a setting with good sun exposure for her flower gardening. After thirty years of marriage, they were content with largely independent lives. Judy's world was centered around flowers and the home, and the social life of her church. Walter's was centered around the office and putting together Oak Harbor's largest and most ambitious development projects.

Much as Walter had made his livelihood in urban development, he was still a country person at heart and preferred to live outside the city, closer to nature. Where else could you wake up to an owl on the roof or a family of barn swallow fledglings lined up on the eave, waiting for breakfast?

When his neighbors mowed their fields, Bald

Eagles and Red-tailed Hawks converged from miles around to circle just over his head, or stand amid the stubble and digest a fat rodent. In the rainy season, Great-blue Herons gathered around the pools that formed in the low spots.

This area near San de Fuca was rich in history, both pre- and post-settlement. Gibbs knew that the Skagit people had lived all around Penn Cove in longhouse settlements, and no doubt had hunted game on his land. People found spear points all over the island, in farmers' fields and backyard gardens. Many island children had begun their education in the one-room San de Fuca schoolhouse, which was still standing.

More important to him, this location also was relatively peaceful, mostly away from the usual flight path of the Navy's Growler jets. That was something he never brought up or mentioned to friends in the business community, who were outspokenly pro-military. He displayed a small, "We Love Jet Noise," sign next to the driveway, but had never gotten used to the shrill roar of the jets. The city, with its fast-food restaurants and box stores, seemed soulless to him.

He thought often of his sister, who had simply disappeared from his life in 2008. Had she given up on him, covered her tracks and walked away from the material life altogether? It was possible – believable. She might be meditating in a monastery right now, somewhere in the mountains of Nepal.

He had wanted nothing so much as to make a success of his life, overcome the poverty that had defined their childhood, and help his sister grow old in comfort. Elliott Langston had nearly prevented his biggest project of all, the Gibbs Addition. Marlene Meyers had saved it but at what cost? He had cast his lot with her and done the unforgivable.

A few miles away at that moment, Coroner Ralph

Emerson was standing at an aluminum exam table, studying the two skeletons, when his clerk dropped the mail in his inbox. He ignored the interruption, took a sip of his latte, set down his cardboard cup and reached for the telephone.

"Kat, you might like to see this," he said. "I can give you a better picture of what happened to your victims now."

"I'm on my way," she replied.

She arrived at his office twenty minutes later and went straight to the basement, where she found him opening the mail.

Dr. Emerson got up and took a position across the table from Kat.

"This is Elliott," he said, pointing at the skeleton on the table. He picked up the skull. "You can see here that the entry wound was right at the back of the skull. The gun must have been touching his head. The bullet passed all the way through and exited here," he said, turning the skull on its side, to reveal a large hole below the lower jaw. The exit wound was massive.

"Luckily, the shot spared most of his teeth, which helped us with dental identification. From the angle of trajectory, I'd say Elliott was on his knees and the killer was standing behind and above him."

"Very professional," Kat said.

"Very. I don't think this was the killer's first time."

"What about the woman?"

Dr. Emerson turned to the other skull.

"Very similar – kneeling. She was shot at point blank range and the bullet exited through the jaw, destroying most of her lower teeth. Neither shot was survivable. One bullet apiece is all it took."

Kat shivered. The two victims knew what was coming. She hoped it had been fast.

"Anything on the DNA yet?" she asked.

"I'm just getting to the mail," Dr. Emerson said. "Let me take a look while you're here."

The stack was about two inches high and she imagined it could take hours to process if it contained anything beyond routine death certificates, lab results and professional mailings. He seemed to know what he was looking for, and put his fingers on a brown manila envelope halfway down in the pile.

He fished it out and slid his letter opener neatly along the flap. Pulling the papers from the envelope, he took a moment to register what he saw.

"Holy cow," he exclaimed. "I've got your Jane Doe, the woman in the sinkhole with Elliott Langston."

"And it is?"

"Someone whose DNA runs in the Gibbs family – it lines up almost point for point with Walter Gibbs's late father. It seems that the father, before his death, submitted a DNA sample to see if he could find any unknown relatives."

"Walter Gibbs has almost no living relatives," Kat remarked. "Maybe none. I think that's what he told me."

"Apparently he had a sister."

"That's right. But he said he lost her a few years ago."

"Do you know how?"

"No, but I'm going to find out."

Back at the Freeland precinct, Kat leaned forward at her computer and studied the aerial image on Google Earth. She zoomed closer to make out the details. She was looking at a suburban neighborhood of modest, older homes with single-car driveways.

The streets were tree-lined and yards were neat and well maintained, but minimal in size. Front lawns were brown, no doubt since water was precious and limited by city ordinance. The area had been in a drought status for years. The particular house that interested her had a small back yard with board fences on both sides separating it from the neighboring houses.

With a name like Gibbs, it hadn't taken Kat long to find where the woman she was seeking had lived – in Visalia, California. But her trail had gone cold in 2008. There was no record she had lived anywhere else in the U.S. after that. The coincidence in timing was stunning. Kat used a locator service to look up the next-door neighbors on both sides of the Gibbs home and called. She got lucky on the second call, reaching a widow named Velma Bachelor, who had lived in her home for thirty years.

"Oh, I remember Patty well," Mrs. Bachelor said. "Lovely girl, very spiritual, never married. She was maybe a little woo-woo, but was like a daughter to me. We talked almost every day on the phone or over the back fence."

"Whatever happened to her?" Kat asked.

"She mentioned she was going out of town for a few days and asked if I'd keep an eye on her house. I had a key. She took a cab to the airport, I guess, because she left her car in the driveway. I don't know where she was going and she never came back."

"You told the police?"

"Yes, after she'd been gone about ten days. They weren't too concerned. I kept calling them back as the days passed. Eventually they investigated her as a missing person but there was no trace – no sign of foul play, no clues on her computer to where she'd gone. If she bought an airline ticket, they said she must have used another name and paid cash. I always had the feeling she was covering her tracks for some reason." Mrs. Bachelor laughed. "I watch too much true crime on TV."

"Did she ever mention a brother on Whidbey Island?"

"Oh yes, Walter the wheeler-dealer real estate developer. She loved him but didn't agree with his values."

"Meaning?"

"Too consumed with the almighty dollar."

"Do you think she was going to see him?"

"Maybe. I don't know. Why keep it a big secret if that's all it was? He came down here and looked for her, went through the house and eventually cleared out all her possessions, and put it on the market. I understand the police talked to him and he didn't know anything about her plans to be gone."

"Do you know if she had any close friends in Visalia, someone in whom she might have confided what was on her mind?"

"Oh gosh, it's been a long time." Mrs. Bachelor went silent for a moment and Kat let her think. "She belonged to a small Buddhist society. I don't know much about it, but she mentioned someone named, what was it? Achara. I think they were friends."

"That's very helpful," Kat said. "I'm afraid I must confirm what you probably already suspect," Kat said. "It appears Patricia was murdered back in 2008 and her remains were buried on Whidbey Island. But please don't discuss this with Walter Gibbs or anyone else till we get further in our investigation. I'll be in touch again when I know more."

*

Patricia Gibbs had left her home in Visalia just before Thanksgiving of 2008 and traveled to Whidbey Island, and ended up dead in a hole under the street with environmental lawyer Elliott Langston.

Walter Gibbs had given a convincing performance when he mentioned how much he missed his sister. Had he murdered her? Or was it possible he didn't even know she was the woman in the hole?

Kat needed to find Achara. A quick online search yielded eight Buddhist temples in the greater Visalia area but only one in Visalia itself. Kat dialed the number and listened to it ring.

The middle-aged woman in blue sat in the lotus position on her cushion, eyes closed, hands together, staring straight ahead in silence as she had been doing for the last half hour. She was trying not to break meditation but could hear a phone ringing softly in another room. After several rings, someone picked it up and spoke a few words, pausing to take a message, and then saying, "I'll have her call back."

When she finished and picked up her cushion, a member of the temple staff approached and told her of the call. A sheriff's deputy, a young-sounding woman from Washington state, wanted to talk with her. Achara found the request baffling, but she was curious.

Kat was alone and deep in thought at her desk in the south precinct office when Shane Lindstrom walked in. "What the ..."

"Oh, sorry," Kat said. "I tracked down Patricia Gibbs's best friend and am waiting for a call back. Got lucky and found the Buddhist association in Visalia. The guy who answered the phone knew her. In fact, she was there at the time, but meditating, and he said he couldn't interrupt her, but she'd call back."

In the corner of the room, on a plush dog bed, sat a black dog with white spots. Shane pointed.

"Is he with you?" Shane asked.

"He is now."

"Is that regulation?"

"It is now."

"You seem a little testy."

"Guy and I are not quite on the same page. I don't need trouble with you on top of it."

Shane arched his eyebrows, opened his mouth as if to speak, but didn't, and turned back to his desk.

*

"Patty!" Achara exclaimed when Kat got the call back and brought up Patricia's name. "It's been so long since I said that name."

"I talked with a former neighbor, a Mrs. Bachelor, who said she thought you were probably Patricia's closest friend."

"Yes, I suppose so. I met her at the temple shortly after we both moved here. She had come out west from North Carolina and done some modeling and acting in Hollywood, and hated the life. I think she and Walter were both trying to find where they fit in the world.

"She drifted around for a while, fell into meditating to reduce the stress in her life, lived in Ojai for a time and ended up buying a house in sleepy Visalia. But what's this about? Why are you bringing up Patty after all these years?"

"I'm afraid we've found her remains," Kat said, "on Whidbey Island. I'm trying to figure out how she got here, and why, and the circumstances of her death."

"So, she didn't die of natural causes?" Achara asked.

"No. But please treat this as confidential while we're still investigating. Please don't share what I'm telling you with anyone else."

Kat heard Achara sniffle and then blow her nose. She gave her a moment.

"Can you tell me anything about what was going on in her life around the time she disappeared?" Kat asked.

"Just that she was lonely. There was always a sadness about her. She and her brother – Walter, I think was his name – had grown up in poverty in the mountains of North Carolina. I don't think she had any other family. Her parents were deceased and she was largely estranged from Walter."

"Did she say what the problem was?"

"They were such opposites – had nothing in common in their values. He had chosen the road of wealth and affluence. She had turned inward and spiritual, and shunned all that. She knew what he was doing on Whidbey Island and it troubled her deeply."

"Do you think that had something to do with her decision to travel to the island?"

"Yes, I'm pretty sure. She said she had to try to stop him. Buddhism teaches a principle called 'right livelihood,' which means exercising moral restraint from various vices of greed and dishonesty that add up to living in a way that harms others."

"Did she say how she was going to stop him?"

"She had information about what he was doing. She said there was a man she wanted to talk to who might be able to use the information to block Walter's ambitions. She never told me who it was. Her dream was to turn Walter around and put him on the road to a more spiritual life."

"Any idea what kind of information she might have had?"

"She didn't say. She was very interested in Native American history and culture – she was part Cherokee, you know. I had the idea this man might share that same interest. There's a big military presence on Whidbey Island and that was another thing – she wasn't very high on the military."

Growlers

"Do you think the murders had anything to do with Elliott's efforts to protect Native American burial grounds in Oak Harbor?" Kat asked her husband. They were pedaling side-by-side next to Crockett Marsh, near the Coupeville ferry terminal.

Traffic on this stretch of highway was light – just the occasional car every few minutes, with lots of room to swing into the oncoming lane. Photographers often stopped their vehicles in the traffic lanes and unrolled their windows to photograph raptors without getting out. Most of the traffic was headed to the ferry landing at Keystone Harbor, where boats left every forty-five minutes for Port Townsend.

From the corner of her eye, Kat watched a female Northern Harrier hover and drop several feet onto an unseen rodent or snake in a clump of grass by the shore of the marsh. She saw harriers on almost every trip to this place and never tired of their swooping and hovering.

"I don't know. It's possible," he said as he reached over his shoulder and adjusted his long, black braid. "But it was so cold-blooded, I think it was carefully planned. I don't think it was done in the heat of the moment."

"Me, neither."

Since marrying Kat and moving to the island, Guy

had landed a coveted job with the county as a marine biologist working in fish restoration. The work gave him access to every pocket estuary and patch of shoreline on the island, and knowledge of how it had once contributed to the vast salmon resource, before the settlers "improved" things by cutting the trees, filling wetlands for agricultural fields and building concrete bulkheads on the fish-breeding substrate.

In the distance, Kat could hear the shrill howl of a military jet approaching low over Admiralty Inlet.

"Growler," Kat said. "It's going to get noisy."

Guy nodded and scowled.

"Plenty of people don't like Indians," he said, "and if they think some Indian-lover environmentalist is standing in the way of progress, that's a potential motive to make him disappear. If he happens to hate Navy jet noise, that's an even bigger motive."

As they pedaled, the Growler came in so low over the beach Kat could see the helmets of the two crew members in the cockpit, visors flashing in the sunlight as they turned their heads right and left. The shriek was so loud now they both stopped their bikes and clamped their hands over their ears. Another was in the pattern a few minutes behind it. They typically trained in twos.

The planes were about to touch and go at the Navy's outlying landing field just through the trees from here, a short runway designed to mimic the deck of an aircraft carrier. After making contact with the runway, they would accelerate to takeoff power and scream even louder as they climbed back into the sky.

Many Coupeville residents hated the Growlers for their treetop-level noise, which often happened at night when people were trying to sleep so they could go to work in the morning, or camping at the nearby parks. Some of those who suffered the most with Growler noise were military veterans who had returned from the war zone with post-traumatic stress damage, desperately needing peace and the soothing presence of nature.

Many in Oak Harbor championed the jets for the economic opportunity they represented, and Kat knew the line between money and patriotism was thin and blurry. Many military veterans retired in Oak Harbor and prospered in the local economy.

The Growler controversy had grown even greater after a big Navy buildup of the jets at the Oak Harbor base and their use of quiet areas in Olympic National Park to conduct electronic warfare training. Since the base was built, each new generation of aircraft seemed to be louder and more intrusive than the last.

"Patricia Gibbs was anti-Growler," Kat said when the noise eased between jets.

"So was Elliott Langston," Guy noted.

"Do you think that brought them together?"

"I'm sure it contributed."

Kat thought about Walter Gibbs. He couldn't possibly be anything but pro-Growler. It was unthinkable not to be a cheerleader for the jet if one were a developer whose fortune depended on continued population growth and economic expansion.

Kat had precious little to tell her why Patricia Gibbs had wanted to meet with Langston. She wondered about the anonymous tip that had led her to Ma Barker. "Talk to Ma Barker. She knows something about it."

Maybe Ma knew more than she had shared in their first meeting.

Fling

Kat inched her cruiser down the rutted gravel lane, easing through soupy potholes, her grille flashers blinking red and blue. It was a misty morning and drizzle kept blurring the view through her windshield. She had the wipers on intermittent. Up ahead, she could see the orange machinery of Ma Barker's logging operation, making fast work of their clearcut.

It had been an unusual summer rain the last couple of days – refreshing but sloppy.

The door of Ma's white pickup opened and the driver's left foot planted itself in the muck. *Practical shoes,* Kat thought. The rest of the stocky woman followed the leg and she stood by the door, walkie-talkie in hand once again.

Kat pulled to a stop, put on her hat, opened her door, and turned her body halfway out, while staying seated. The smell of diesel permeated the clearing.

"Morning," Kat said.

"Back at ya," Ma replied. "Kinda hoped I had seen the last of you."

"Oh now, let's not get off on the wrong foot. I'm just looking for a little chat. Hop in out of the rain."

"Who's the civilian?" Ma asked, pointing at the polka dot face behind the protective steel grill.

"Duncan. My new partner."

"Well, isn't he a cutie! Specially trained?"

"Untrained, but sincere."

"Well, there aren't any bodies buried around this property if that's why you brought him," Ma said.

Kat explained she was still digging into the murder of Elliott Langston and a female companion whose remains were found in the hole with him. "I don't know who killed him or why, but the pieces are starting to come together."

"Well, much as he made my life miserable, he didn't deserve what happened."

"That's a remarkably charitable attitude."

"Well, that's me, too soft for my own good."

Kat smiled. "I received an interesting, anonymous tip about the investigation. 'Talk to Ma Barker. She knows something about it.' What do you think the caller meant by that?"

"Oh boy, I really didn't want to go into this," Ma said, shaking her head from side to side. Raindrops dripped off her hat as she spoke. "Elliott and I had a little fling a few months before he disappeared."

Kat's face froze. "How is that even *possible*?"

"You know, opposites..."

"A tree hugger and a clearcutter? How did that go?" Kat was genuinely curious now.

"Well, I think he was trying to figure me out, and I was doing the same with him. I can still pour on the charm when I get the hormones fired up. Give me credit, I'm voluptuous," she laughed. "I thought maybe I could get on his good side and figure out a way to coexist with him on this island. You know, maybe we didn't have to step on each others' toes all the time."

"Was he a good lover?" Kat instantly regretted the unprofessional question. "I apologize. I'm way out of line."

"I've had worse," Ma said, not batting an eye.

"So did you find out what he was working on?"

"I know he had a source who was feeding him information about Marlene Meyers and Elliott Gibbs.

They both took a lot of shortcuts to get what they wanted. Elliott's source seemed to know a lot of history that wasn't part of the public record."

"Do you think the woman in the hole was his source?"

"Oh yeah."

"Any idea how this source got her information?"

"Elliott led me to believe she came upon boxes of old files when cleaning out a deceased relative's home. I think it was papers one or the other of them didn't want in the public records – didn't want stored where they could be found in a county office or professional building. So, they hauled them home and kept them in the closet."

"What does your gut tell you about the killer? Who do you think did this?"

"I honestly don't know. From what I read, he was about as cold-blooded as it gets."

"Were their interests pretty entangled – Walter and Marlene?"

"What do you think? Marlene wanted those houses built. She had a big financial stake in Walter's project."

"And you?"

Ma smiled. "I just cut trees."

Where the Skagits Lived

It was Kat's idea for Guy and *Duncan* to come with her on a walk around Oak Harbor Bay and lower Old Town on Saturday. "All three of us need the exercise, and it'll be a good opportunity for you to tell me what you know about the city's native history," she said. She knew Guy's work for the county had given him a good understanding of the native lifestyle on Whidbey. In the back of her mind, Kat felt Elliott Langston's murder had something to do with the collision of native and Western values. Of course, she also had a secret agenda, which was to give Guy some bonding time with *Duncan*.

Guy suggested they park at Scenic Heights and walk all three sides of Oak Harbor Bay to where the trail ends across from downtown. That way they could see it all. They parked, clipped a leash to *Duncan's* collar, and started to walk. He had already found something at trailside to investigate with his polka dot nose. After a moment he raised his head high in the air and inhaled – a handsome boy.

"Coming down this hillside, we're entering what's called Freund Marsh," Guy said. It's part of the 320-acre Donation Land Claim settled by Ulrich Freund in 1850. He was one of the three original white settlers whose arrival began the displacement of the Skagit people from the bay. By then smallpox from early encounters with traders had already devastated the native population."

"It's beautiful," Kat said, noticing the native vegetation and listening to the birdsong, especially the metallic notes of the Red-winged Blackbirds clinging to cattails in the marsh. A striped female perched nearby with a big insect in its mouth – a beakful of arms and legs -- waiting for a safe moment to dash to its nest in the reeds. A blue dragonfly zipped past Kat's head. She stopped to read several interpretive signs describing the birds and vegetation of the land, and smiled at couples walking briskly for exercise, with their children and dogs.

"What brought the settlers to Oak Harbor?" Kat asked.

"They had come up empty in the California Gold Rush and were looking for free 'government' land – Ulrich Freund, Martin Toftezen and Charlie Sumner. Ironically, to get here they hired native crews with canoes to provide their transportation. The natives inadvertently participated in their own near-extinction.

"The whole area around this bay was quite different back in those days," Guy continued. "It was a prairie and looked like the easiest, choicest land to farm. When Freund settled on this stretch of the shore, he drained the wetlands and converted them to farmland. Now, one hundred fifty years later, the city is restoring Freund's land to a more natural state so it can serve as a buffer between downtown and the bay, and filter the polluted runoff from urban streets and parking lots that would otherwise enter the bay here."

As they continued to walk, they came to Windjammer Park and the center of the bay downtown. "Charlie Sumner settled this next piece, which became the city beach and playground, and Martin Toftezen claimed the easternmost section, where Old Town and the native burials are located."

Kat spotted someone kneeling in the distance, in

a familiar safari hat. "Let me introduce you to someone," she told her husband.

"This is Don Mosier, the city archaeologist," Kat said when they reached his location. He was standing next to a backhoe that was digging the foundation for a new picnic shelter. Guy shook his hand.

"You're the guardian of our Skagit burials," Guy said. "I'm pleased to meet you. I'm not Salish but I do care a lot that our ancestors are treated with respect."

Mosier smiled. "I try not to get caught off guard by digging in this part of town, but am still surprised by what turns up, and where. Those two skeletons in the sinkhole a while back really threw me."

"No one could have foreseen that," Kat said.

"Well, after the excitement settled, we got the street repaved and the merchants are happy again. For once the holdup wasn't native burials, but perhaps this served as a reminder that all human remains, whatever their origin, deserve our respect. The remains of native people shouldn't be valued any less than those of non-natives. How is your investigation going, by the way?"

"Making good progress," Kat replied. "We're going to find out who did it."

She and Guy said their goodbyes and went back to their walk. They were now nearly to the gate of the Navy's Seaplane Base.

Guy explained that William Maylor bought land on what's called Maylor Point and farmed it until the Navy arrived and needed it to build a base for its Catalina flying boats, the principal antisubmarine aircraft of World War II.

"Many native graves were located on this piece, which stretches from Old Town around the bay to Crooked Spit," he said. "The spit extended most of the way from Maylor Point across to what's now downtown Oak Harbor. The Navy dredged away most of the spit and relocated the native remains to La Conner. By

1942, this was a Navy base."

"Hard to believe everything changed so much, so fast," Kat said.

Guy added, "I get so frustrated that when you read about the history of places like this, it starts with the arrival of the settlers in the 1850s. That's just not true at all. Human history here goes back thousands of years. Native history was oral – passed down through storytelling. If we're going to talk about history, let's try to tell the whole story."

The morning's walk had taken Kat, Guy and *Duncan* all the way onto Navy land at Maylor Point, where the public is allowed to use a walking trail. They were looking across the bay now to downtown Oak Harbor, and Kat pictured in her mind the prairie savannah that once sprawled across the hillside where tourist shops, restaurants, bookstores and taverns now stood.

She imagined Garry Oak trees, and wildflowers, and deer, and longhouses. It must have been a paradise on earth for hundreds, if not thousands, of years. No wonder reformers such as Elliott Langston mourned what had been lost, and wanted to save and restore some of the original beauty and unique character of this place.

Balance

"Marlene Meyers is on Facebook," Kat remarked as she looked up from her computer at the office. Shane looked over her way.

"Learning anything?" he asked.

"She's a piece of work. But I need a new computer."

"What's wrong with that one?"

"Nothing. I mean I need a new one at home. I could do some of this research on my own time there. My old laptop barely boots up anymore."

"How is it going with Guy and the dog?"

"The dog is winning. I walked in the other evening and caught Guy rolling on the floor with him. Fun to see Guy lose some of his dignity. He takes this Native American stuff seriously – always feels like he has to be perfect and more professional than any of his Anglo counterparts."

"You seem more settled these days," Shane remarked.

"I think *Duncan* is bringing some balance to my life. We take walks. We hang out on the beach. He finds stuff and makes me smile. I relax and forget the job for a few hours. I want him to have a good life after all the turmoil of his early years."

"I'm seeing some parallels to your years as a homeless teen in the Adirondacks. Rescuing *Duncan*, maybe it's your way of paying things forward."

"Maybe. Everyone deserves a chance. I think *Duncan* was abused as a young dog."

"What makes you say that?"

"He cringes if someone walks toward him with an object – like a stick or a broom. The ears go back and his tail drops. His lips curl and you can see a few teeth. He's afraid. I think someone beat him or chased him with a stick or tool."

"How can people be so cruel?"

Kat turned back to her computer. "Marlene lives in Tulare now. Isn't that just down the road from Visalia, where Patricia Gibbs lived?"

"Yeah."

Kat scrolled back though her posts. "She's a conspiracy theorist and ultra right-winger."

The more Kat learned about Marlene, the more intrigued she grew with a possible connection to the murders. She was just about to dig deeper into Marlene's Facebook account when the telephone rang. It was Don Mosier, the archaeologist.

"I've been thinking about those skeletons we recovered," Mosier said. "It finally hit me they were buried in a particular type of fill different from what's in the rest of the hole. Sediments are sort of a hobby of mine," he explained.

"So, what can you tell me?" Kat asked.

"The gravels of Central Whidbey are the products of glaciation. In the last big event of the Ice Age, the Vashon Glacier came down from the north and left north-south striations all over Whidbey Island and Puget Sound. You can see them clearly on Lidar maps that strip away the vegetation and just show the Earth."

"Okay."

"But Central Whidbey and Penn Cove were also shaped by a lobe of ice that came down the Skagit River in a northwest-to-southeast direction."

"And this means?"

"When a glacier stops advancing, it drops the load of rock it is carrying. That ice left some nice deposits of gravel that has been quarried for years, but it has a distinct character. When I looked around the hole at the area where we dug out the skeletons, it's as if there'd been one truckload of gravel dumped with them that was distinctly different from everything else. Historically, much of it was mined from a now-abandoned quarry north of Oak Harbor.

"There's another thing, too," he said. "I found some preserved organic material – bits of twigs and buds – mixed in with the gravel. It turned out to be native rhododendrons, and the quarry I'm thinking of is overrun with them. If I were you, I think I'd take a hard look around that site."

A Forgotten Place

Kat released the rusty chain and pulled onto the weedy, disused gravel road. The old quarry was one of several on north Whidbey that fit a picture of the probable murder site she'd been developing in her mind. Years ago it had been an active gravel-mining site. But with the shifting economy, limited supply and emergence of larger, more convenient quarries, it had been abandoned.

Kat needed a murder scene. She had the bodies. She knew who they were. She knew they'd been kneeling when shot from behind at point-blank range. She had several suspects with a motive to kill. She had a theory on how the victims were transported to their final resting place, with a load of gravel in the back of a truck. But she did not know *where* they were murdered. And all these years later, it would be a miracle if she could find any physical evidence.

The murders could have been done at Elliott Langston's modular home in the woods, but Roger had investigated that scene thoroughly after Langston's disappearance and found only a few cigarette butts. More likely, the murders took place somewhere else, where the killer knew he'd have privacy, no one would look, a staging area for transporting the bodies to the Old Town dig.

Tall grass and huckleberry branches raked the

side of Kat's cruiser as she proceeded to the clearing. It was well concealed off the road, a good place that surely afforded privacy. No homes were close enough to hear any shots. She rolled to a stop in the clearing, shut off the engine, opened the door and got out. Kat stood there and arched her back to stretch, and looked around. Rhododendrons were everywhere, as Mosier had said.

The once-active pit was now just a resting place for rusty machinery and piles of garbage. Broken glass littered the ground. Someone had been target-shooting beer bottles, and there were dozens of shell casings. Off toward the edge of the clearing, an old hulk caught her eye, and she walked over.

It was the remains of a panel van someone had burned long ago. There were plenty of these old hulks in the woods, abandoned and rusting or burned by owners after they stopped running. The doors were rusted shut and the dash was just metal and wires. The tires had melted down to the rims. All the windows were broken. Kat leaned through the driver's window and looked for a vehicle identification number, but could see none. Both license plates were gone. Had it been abandoned here by its owner? Maybe. Stolen? Possibly. Used in a crime? She might never know, but if it had, burning it would go a long way to erase any evidence.

Near as she could tell, it was a Ford Econoline van, a popular model that had been built and sold from the 1960s on. She noted the cargo bay was windowless, which made this a realistic choice for a tradesman, or if someone were transporting people or cargo they wanted no one else to see. There had been a roof rack where someone must have once attached ladders, lumber, pipe or conduit. She took a few photographs on her cell phone to jog her memory later, when she got back to the office.

She had a feeling about this place. She would

visit a few other likely spots in the nearby area, but this had all the elements.

"I've got to dash home for a few minutes," Kat told Shane when she got back to the office. "FedEx is delivering my new laptop today and I've got to sign for it."

Kat was just fixing an egg salad sandwich in the kitchen when she heard the 'beep, beep' of the delivery van. She had let *Duncan* out to sit on the porch and get some air, but didn't want to leave him alone to greet the driver. She was still getting to know his ways. Kat put down her sandwich and rushed to the door, but the FedEx driver, a young woman, was faster and was already on the porch. *Duncan* had moved off about twenty feet and was watching, ears back, lips curled.

"I think he got me," the woman said, handing Kat the box with the computer.

"What? Who?" Kat replied.

"Your dog. He nipped me in the heel."

"Are you okay? He's new and I had no idea. Did he break the skin?"

"I don't think so."

"Let's see," Kat said.

The driver lifted her pant leg. A rivulet of bright, red blood ran down her heel and into her shoe.

"Oh no," Kat said. "Sit down here on the bench while I put him in the house. She put a leash on *Duncan* and led him inside. "Let me get you an antiseptic and a bandage."

"I love dogs," the driver said. "He caught me by surprise."

"We had a little incident today," Kat told Guy when he got home. *"Duncan* bit the FedEx girl."

"What?" Guy asked emphatically.

"He was fast. I didn't see it happen but it's my fault for not putting him in the house before she got here. I patched her up and suggested she see a doctor to have the wound cleaned and get a shot. I told her we'll pay any bills."

"Oh, that's just great. So, we've got a biter. That's going to be an expensive computer."

"I think he was just afraid. She was carrying a box and it may have looked like a threat to him."

"We can't have a dog that bites."

"I'm going to see somebody about him. Give me a chance. There may be something we can do."

Probation

"How's that new dog working out for you?" Shane asked the next morning when Kat arrived at work.

"Not so good. He and I are on probation at the moment. He bit the FedEx girl."

"Oh no!" Shane replied, shaking his head. "Did she do something to upset him?"

"Just carried a package containing my computer from the truck to the porch. I meant to put him in the house but she was a little too fast for me, getting the box out of the truck. Guy wants *Duncan* gone when he gets home tonight. Maybe he's right. Things are pretty frosty between us right now. Guy's under pressure at work. I'm looking for a last-ditch way to buy *Duncan* some time while I figure out what to do."

"There is a woman – I'll look up her name – who specializes in reprogramming dogs that are fearful and reactive to certain triggers. I've heard she is quite good."

"I need the name fast," Kat said. "I didn't adopt *Duncan* just to become a dog-murderer. But I also need something else. Tell me what Marlene Meyers did and how county government works. If she's involved somehow in Elliott Langston's murder, I need to know what her powers were during the years she was a county commissioner."

"That's a little more than I'm qualified to do, but

there is a former state legislator who lives out by Bush Point. He knows the ins and outs of government. I'll put you in touch. In fact, I think you already know him, one of our citizens' patrol volunteers, R.P. Beath."

"The metal-detector guy?"

"That's him."

Beath had been impressive in one of Kat's earlier cases, finding a critical piece of evidence with a metal detector in the shallows of Useless Bay. It was a missing cell phone from which they recovered key data. She had no idea he'd served in the legislature, as well. But people who had an ethic of public service keep a low profile and go on finding ways to serve even in retirement.

Kat headed out Smugglers Cove Road from Freeland and found Beath's home at the end of a winding lane, high on a bluff, overlooking Admiralty Inlet and Marrowstone Island a few miles across the water. It was a stunning location from which he could watch the constant activity in the Puget Sound shipping lanes, including the passage of nuclear submarines headed to and from their base at Bangor, on Hood Canal. A huge nuclear weapons depot on Indian Island supported those submarines. It was tucked just inside Marrowstone.

She knocked and he answered the door, shaking hands with her warmly. "Come in, come in. Good to see you again." He led her to a table and resin chairs on the deck facing the water.

"This view just takes my breath away," Kat said. Right now, she was looking at a tug pushing a barge full of gravel, and containerships passing in both directions.

"I like ships. There's always something to see out here. Of course, big storms are the best."

Kat waited a moment while they both watched the scene. Nothing she'd experienced as a homeless teen in the Adirondacks prepared her for a view like this.

FINAL COVER-UP

Puget Sound was a world apart. Finally, she began, "My boss tells me you can explain county government to me."

Beath laughed.

"Shane? He's one of the good guys. I tried to talk him into running for the legislature but he wanted no part of it – all that knocking on doors and fundraising, campaign signs, coffee hours. I don't blame him. He loves what he's doing.

"But as to your question, it isn't too complicated. Most of the counties in Washington are smaller in population and are organized as non-charter counties. They're governed by three elected commissioners who make decisions by majority rule. It's the oldest form of government in the United States, by the way, going all the way back to colonial times.

"They have authority to enact ordinances, set budgets, oversee hiring, a whole bunch of things. These days it's the environmental piece and land-use planning that's often the most complicated for them, complying with the state's Growth Management Act. It gets interesting because, with the demographic differences in various parts of the county, the commissioners are often a mix of conservatives and liberals, and they have to work together."

"That's what I'm wondering about," Kat said. "There was a commissioner a few years ago, Marlene Meyers, who apparently rocked the boat pretty hard on environment and development."

"You think?" Beath asked. "She was pushing a big expansion of home-building in Oak Harbor. More homes, of course, means more demand for box stores, parking lots and fast-food franchises. She made her name as wildly anti-environment and wouldn't leave office when she lost reelection. Wore a sidearm to council meetings and intimidated her fellow commissioners. She called them anti-Navy, unpatriotic, anti-progress, tree-huggers who ought to be shot. She made her contempt clear about the Salish burial ground in Oak Harbor's Old Town. A lot of people agreed with her."

Until now, Kat had wondered if Marlene Meyers was directly responsible for the murders. Now she realized there was another possibility. Marlene may have incited someone else to act, thinking it was his patriotic duty.

"The calls for violence were the scary part," Beath said. "You could say it was just bluster, but when you talk like that, you never know what impact your words are having. Is it just colorful language or a call to action? You can embolden unstable people to take the law into their own hands and resort to violence. Her people were worked up, feeling invincible. Some of them organized truck parades and drove around with red-and-black "Meyers" flags flying from their vehicles. She stirred up a whole hornet's nest of angry followers who came close to shutting down county government."

"Why?"

"I always felt it was a personal power trip. She craved attention. She was a narcissist who knew how to push people's buttons and inflame a crowd. Crooked as hell. She was profiting from office, and the Navy, and had designs to stay in her job and make a lot more in future dealings."

"How was she finally pushed out if she wouldn't go voluntarily?"

"Elections have to be certified by the county canvassing board, which in our case is the county auditor, the county prosecutor and the chair of the county commissioners. They certified her opponent as the winner, and when Marlene challenged it, a judge upheld the canvassing board's decision. That took courage and he received death threats. In fact, the police tracked down the caller and prosecuted him. In the end, she didn't have a leg to stand on."

Kat shook her head. "How did the courthouse

conflict finally end?"

"Police and national guard threw a perimeter around the courthouse and confronted Marlene's mob. The new commissioner was sworn in. Marlene finally announced she was going off to California to organize a larger political movement and would be back when the time was right."

Kat needed to find out who was arrested and charged during the Meyers uproar. Identifying the most radical members of the movement might lead her to a suspect. She also needed to know what Meyers was doing these days and the extent of her continuing involvement in county development. She thanked Beath and headed back to her office.

Hours later, after some work at the computer, she had compiled a list of fourteen persons of interest. One of them was Marvin Trammel, Langston's neighbor, who had been arrested after using his equipment to remove barricades in front of the county courthouse on the day Marlene's people tried to breach the building.

"I was swept up in the heat of the moment," Trammel said when Kat called him. "We thought we were doing the right thing, but with the clarity of hindsight, I regret it now."

Several military and ex-military personnel participated in that incident. None remained on active duty all these years later as far as Kat could tell.

The highest profile leader in Marlene's movement was a well-known Oak Harbor conservative named Larry Ward.

Larry Ward

Kat found the Larry Ward home on a hilltop in Oak Harbor's Scenic Heights neighborhood, overlooking Oak Harbor Bay. It was a tidy rambler with a well-groomed yard, a large U.S. flag flying from a pole by the street, and a Dodge Ram 4x4 pickup parked in the driveway. She noted a gun rack in the rear window and a "Support Our Troops" bumper sticker, in addition to a faded "Meyers" sticker. A yard sign proclaimed, "We Love Jet Noise."

A computer search back at Kat's office had identified Ward as the man who was prosecuted for the death threats against the county judge. News articles at the time characterized him as a leader of Marlene's movement. He was high-profile and outspoken, the author of numerous letters to the editor denouncing the Growler opponents and what he saw as the county's left-wing leadership.

Kat knocked on the front door. When it opened, she was looking at a tall, slim man with a bald head, seventy-some years old. She could tell from his build he had been very fit as a younger man.

"Larry Ward?" she asked.

"That's right."

"Could I come in and chat with you for a few minutes?"

Without comment, he stepped back so she could

enter and showed her to a chair in the living room. This was obviously a man's house, rather Spartan with none of the usual feminine touches, framed photographs, art or decorations. But she did note some military memorabilia – a pistol in a glass case, a torn and blackened Iraqi flag and a black-and-white photograph of several men next to a Humvee.

"Is this you in the picture?" she asked.

"Yes. In Tikrit, Saddam Hussein's birthplace."

"You've seen some of the world."

She explained she was looking into the events of 2008, when activist lawyer Elliott Langston was murdered.

"So, what has this got to do with me?" Ward asked.

"You were prominent in Marlene Meyers's movement and served time for a death threat against a judge who upheld the election of her opponent."

"That judge – the whole election – was crooked. The judge was scum. But I served my time. It's ancient history now."

"Are you still in touch with Marlene Meyers?"

"What are you driving at? Do I need a lawyer?"

"Not at all. This is just a friendly discussion." She smiled.

"I'm still committed to her movement. She'll be back one of these days, stronger than ever."

"I understand you served in Special Forces in the Middle East."

"That's right."

"And after that, as a civilian security contractor for a mercenary organization. Kat watched his eyes, which were darting as she asked her questions.

"That's right – providing security for buildings and vehicles, evading improvised explosive devices and doing some interrogations of terrorist suspects."

"So, you might have known other contractors who did similar work, who lived on the island then or now."

"I might."

"Were any of them involved in the movement?"

"There was a lot of support for Marlene across the board – police, military, business interests. She has a lot of friends. I knew her all the way back to high school. Lots of patriotic people were involved one way or another."

"Would any of them have felt strongly enough to harm Elliott Langston?"

"You'd have to ask them. I will say there wasn't much love for the guy."

Ward was revealing as little as possible, but he was fidgeting, rubbing his thumbs together.

"As you know, Langston and a young woman were murdered and dumped in a hole in the street in Old Town. I imagine it unfolded like some of the disappearances that happen in Third World countries. Maybe you can help me visualize how Special Forces or civilian contractors could make someone disappear without leaving a trace."

"That would be total speculation on my part."

"Well," Kat said, "I'm picturing an unmarked vehicle, maybe stolen. Someone picks up the victims and takes them to a secure location, where any evidence would be hard to trace. Two quick bullets do the job. The bodies are then transported to the disposal site, perhaps in a load of gravel. Does that sound about right?"

"It's plausible. It's one scenario," he said, shifting in his chair.

"The thing is, I think I have found the murder site and the vehicle. I can't help wondering was it a conspiracy?" Did the killer act on his own or at someone else's direction? And who transported the bodies to the street?

Larry didn't respond. Kat's questions seemed to send his thoughts to some faraway place.

Kat's speculation about a conspiracy and acting at someone else's direction had taken him back to that night in 1965.

The car, Ryan's car, was a dual-exhaust fifty-seven Chevy Bel Air. With Ryan at the wheel, it was speeding down West Beach Road, fishtailing from side to side in the darkness and rain. Wind and spray lashed the road. There were four boys in the car and Ryan was practicing skids between swigs of beer. West Beach Road was popular for this. Empty bottles rolled and clinked on the back seat floor, in front of the two passengers back there.

"Cool!" one of the boys in back said.

"Watch this!" Ryan exclaimed.

"You're going too fast," Larry warned, putting his beer between his knees and bracing himself against the dash as he was thrown back and forth. "If you put this car in the ditch, we're going to have some explaining to do."

"You worry too much," Ryan said. "I've got everything under control." He pressed the pedal to the floor, turned the wheel all the way left and sent the car into a three-sixty on the slick pavement. The headlights flashed across something dark in the road and the rear end hit it as it spun around. They all felt a sickening thump.

"What was that, a deer?" Larry asked.

"Who knows?" Ryan said.

"We've got to stop," Larry insisted."

"No way!" Ryan said.

"What if it wasn't a deer?"

Ryan stopped in the road, and reversed and turned around so the headlights illuminated what he'd just hit, something dark by the shoulder. Then he slumped forward over the steering wheel to rest. Larry opened his door, got out and walked back. He knew before he reached the object that it was a person. He bent down to look, then stood and hurried back to the car.

"You hit somebody," he said, shaking so hard he could barely get the words out.

"What?" Ryan said, raising his head from where he was resting it on the steering wheel.

"It's Christy Morris," Larry told him.

"What?"

"Christy Morris from school."

"Is she okay?" Ryan asked.

"No, she's dead."

"She can't be. What was she doing in the middle of the road in the middle of the night?" Ryan asked.

"I don't know but she lives around here someplace. And she's dead," he repeated.

"Oh god," Ryan said. "Oh god, oh god." He was shaking violently now, pounding the wheel and breathing hard. "What are we going to do?"

Larry thought for a moment. "Put her in the trunk."

Ryan and the other boys got out. One of them turned away and threw up his beer. Then, together, the four boys lifted her into the trunk and closed it.

"Mr. Ward?" Kat asked. "Mr. Ward, did I lose you there?" Kat brought Larry back to the present. "If the murders were ordered by someone, I've found that people usually talk sooner or later to save their own skins. So, if you think of anything that might help me, please be in touch. You might be doing us both a favor."

Kat handed him her card. She had accomplished what she came here to do.

Flying the Flag

Marlene Meyers sat at her desk in an upscale Tulare office park and listened to the flag clanging on the pole outside. At twenty by thirty-eight feet, it was the largest flag in Tulare and had cost her a thousand dollars.

She had spent the last hour on the computer, reviewing her income from the Gibbs Addition in Oak Harbor. Walter Gibbs called it his cash cow, and Marlene had to admit that summed it up.

This, plus ongoing political contributions from her mass mailings to Meyers Party followers, meant she was accumulating a sizable war chest for the political battles ahead. With her big smile, movie-star blond hair and confident demeanor, she felt she had a good shot at a seat in the California legislature. With the help of plastic surgery, she was remarkably youthful and pretty for her age. But she was getting up in years and didn't have much time to carry out her dream, if it was going to happen at all.

Her followers loved her feisty rhetoric, calling the Democratic Party the "walking dead" and the governor depraved human scum who panders to addicts, illegal aliens and gays. What really got them stirred up was when she singled out specific politicians in her speeches and tweets, saying it was time to "string them up." They also loved how she trashed the media, mocked the disabled and called for an end to expensive special education programs that do nothing to change reality.

Her exit from Whidbey Island had come fast after she lost the county election. She had chosen Tulare for her new base in view of its reputation as a red county in a blue state. California was so screwed up. Where better than Tulare to launch her march to the legislature of this disastrous, failed state?

A call on Marlene's cell phone brought her out of her thoughts.

"Marlene, it's Larry, how are you?"

"I'm doing great, Larry," she replied.

"Listen," he said, "I thought you should know the sheriff has reopened the Langston case. Maybe you heard they found his body, and that of a woman, under the street in Old Town. A female cop, a young lightweight named Brown, has been snooping around, asking questions."

"Anything that should concern us?" Marlene asked.

"Hard to say. She seems to be putting together a scenario and talking to a lot of people. Says she thinks she found where the murders took place, and the vehicle in which Langston and the woman were transported. I don't know if she's just blowing smoke.

"She also asked about any military contractors I might know who would be experienced in carrying out operations like the Langston disappearance. I thought you should be aware she's poking around."

"Well, please keep me updated if you hear anything more."

Marlene hit "end" and put down the phone. Langston was ancient history. It was hard to believe the sheriff's department would put much time or energy into such a cold case. She wondered who this young female deputy was, and how much she had to prove.

FINAL COVER-UP

*

Kat drove back to Freeland, satisfied she had made an impression on Ward. If he knew anything about the murders, he'd be talking to others involved and thinking about his options. The cold case was heating up.

She called the office and reported where she was, and that she'd be clocking out, taking a long lunch, to deal with some personal business at home. She had arranged to meet the dog behaviorist to evaluate whether *Duncan* could overcome his fears and learn not to bite. Kat got to the house, unlocked the door, let *Duncan* out to sit on the porch, and waited.

Kat was watching out the window when Linda Harrod drove up. She was right on time and parked on the street. When she opened her car door, *Duncan* raised his head and watched. His ears shifted back. Kat was getting nervous. He had already bitten one visitor. She couldn't afford to have him bite another.

"Let me call him inside," Kat said.

"No, let me watch him. His ears are back. I think I know what he's going to do."

Linda walked toward the house, hand in her pocket, never taking her eyes off *Duncan,* who never took his eyes off her. As she got closer, he stepped off the porch and began to circle behind her at a safe distance. He was making a cowardly approach. Linda pulled her hand from her pocket and tossed him a few bacon treats, which stopped him in his tracks. He sniffed and ate them. She had his attention now and tossed several more through the open door of the house. *Duncan* bounded up the steps to find the bacon.

"He was getting into position to take a run at my heels," Linda said. "But when I tossed him the treats, I went from being a threat to something positive. I can work with this dog. He's a good dog. It'll just take some patience and consistency on your part. We'll put him through some exercises with people carrying lumber and brooms on which we've placed treats, so he associates those objects with rewards rather than fear."

It struck Kat that aggression – biting – was really just the flip side of fear. The most dangerous and unstable dogs, Linda said, were those that lacked confidence and were fearful. So a big part of her job was helping dogs get over their fears. Body language was a dead giveaway to what they were thinking.

Kat suspected fear was behind much human behavior as well. It causes unstable people to lash out violently, thinking it's the only way they can gain control of a threat. If you want to get someone to do something reckless or illegal, fan their fears. It was the mainstay of talk radio, after all!

An hour later, *Duncan* and Kat were finished with their first session with Linda. It had gone well and *Duncan* loved all the attention and treats. It looked like Linda was his new best friend.

Kat was headed out the door, on her way back to see Marvin Trammel again.

Kat found Trammel in his garage, on his back, on a creeper he had rolled underneath his backhoe. When his eyes noticed Kat's feet standing nearby, he rolled out and sat up. He was holding a grease gun and had smudges of oil or grease on his face. He reached for a roll of paper towels lying next to the machine, tore off a couple of squares and dipped them into a margarine tub with some gasoline in it. He daubed gasoline on his gooey hands and cleaned the grease from them.

"What can I do for you, officer Brown?" he asked.

"I wanted to talk a little more about your neighbor," Kat said. "When I was here before, you didn't mention you'd been active in Marlene Meyers's movement back in 2008."

"You didn't ask. And it didn't have anything to do with Elliott anyway."

"I'm not so sure. You and he would have been on opposite sides of that conflict."

"As we were on almost everything," Trammel said.

"That movement got pretty militant – emotions ran high. Can you think of someone who might have felt strongly enough to murder your neighbor and his companion?"

"Murder is a pretty big step."

"Especially the kind of murders carried out in this case," Kat said. "They were very professionally done. It makes me think the killer had a lot of experience and perhaps was hired to do it."

"I don't know. I've never thought about it."

"One of the mysteries in this case is the lack of a crime scene," Kat said. "I don't think the murders were carried out next door, though it's possible the victims were kidnapped there."

"Oh," Trammel said.

"I think they were transported somewhere else where they were murdered, and I think I've discovered where."

Trammel's expression turned serious.

"After they were murdered, someone, probably with a gravel truck, moved the bodies to the site in Old Town where they were dumped into the hole. You were one of the contractors working on that project."

"That's true, but so were some other people."

"Well, it's just a question now of finding someone who's willing to tell us the details to save his own skin. By the way, I noticed there were some soldiers involved in the assault on the courthouse. Did you know any of them?"

"No one comes to mind off hand."

"Well, think about it, and if you can help me in any way, give me a call." She handed him her card, turned, got into her car and drove away.

Trammel waited a few minutes, then reached for his jacket on the seat of the front loader, fished his cell phone out of the pocket, and dialed.

"It's Marvin," he said. "We've got a problem."

"What kind of problem?" asked a male voice.

"A sheriff's deputy. She's digging into the Langston case."

"She's got nothing. Let her dig for all the good it will do her."

"Well, this hits a little close to home for me, you know."

"Just keep your mouth shut and everything will be okay."

"But somebody else knows ... She already brought up the possibility that, hypothetically, I was in a position to have done the trucking in this case."

"Just relax and play it straight. Don't let her get to you. It's all hypothetical and that's as far as it's going to go. This is a dead-end case."

Zealots

Kat sat at her desk and twirled a lock of her shoulder-length hair as she studied her list of persons of interest, the most vocal and high-profile leaders of Marlene's movement. One arm of her "Marie Martin" designer sunglasses dangled from her mouth. She was looking for police and military people in the group that had stormed the county courthouse when Marlene lost re-election.

Several of the movement's leaders had been arrested and held briefly, and were named in sheriff's reports.

Five were police officers or had ties to the military or mercenary organizations. Two were deceased. Most had been in their sixties in 2008. Now, they'd be about seventy plus years old, moving into the last chapter of their lives. Two others lived out-of-state, to the extent Kat could find current addresses. It appeared one of the leaders with military experience was living in Greenbank, Ryan Ashford, who had told officers at the time he was a former special forces operator now working for a mercenary organization. It wasn't much, but better than nothing. Sooner or later, she'd find someone who knew something.

Kat swung by her house and picked up *Duncan*. He might as well ride along with her – the socialization was valuable, and Greenbank was a good place for a dog. She loaded her pockets with dog treats, in case he'd need some positive reinforcement. Neither Shane nor the sheriff needed to know. Besides, she had no idea what she'd find when she drove up to Ashford's house. A dog would give her an extra edge if Ashford turned out to be hostile.

If Ashford or some other zealot like him was the shooter, the big question was whether he acted alone or was hired to do it. Walter Gibbs and Marlene Meyers were at the top of Kat's list. More and more, she believed several people were involved and they had kept their mouths shut for more than a decade.

The Bomb

Ashford had replayed his last day in Iraq hundreds of times in his mind. As security officer for the convoy, he was sitting in the right-hand seat of the lead vehicle, beside the driver. They were just approaching the city after an early-morning drive from the airport when he noticed something by the roadside up ahead.

"Better hold up right here while I check this out," he said. The vehicle's headlights were illuminating a shape on the roadside that didn't belong. Night was giving way to dawn and traffic was still very light on the main highway from Baghdad Airport to the city. After an overnight low in the mid-seventies this would be a brutally hot day to wear body armor, forecast for 107 degrees.

The driver stopped the armored vehicle fifty feet from the object. It appeared to be a small gas can left on the road shoulder, and Ashford got out to approach the object. It could be innocent enough, forgotten after someone ran out of gas and put a spare gallon into their tank to get them to a gas station. But they couldn't afford to assume that.

Body armor offered a degree of protection in these ambiguous situations, but not enough. This country and everyone in it was insane.

Ashford looked around for a concealed position from which an insurgent with a transmitter could detonate the device, but saw none. The terrain was flat, and this might be totally innocent. Nevertheless, he was nervous and carried his automatic weapon at the ready, finger on the trigger, and safety switched off. In the back seat of the vehicle, two CIA officers and a third paramilitary waited and watched. The CIA men had just touched down at the airport and were on their way to join their colleagues in the city. A second armored vehicle carrying four additional paramilitaries and their weapons waited behind them.

Objects on the roadway like this sometimes were intended to kill and other times were quite harmless, placed there simply to disrupt and delay American military operations, and erode morale. Ever since the nine-eleven attack on the World Trade Center and the invasion of Iraq, this country had become a quagmire for Americans. In addition to active-duty forces, the U.S. had poured private contractors and mercenaries into Iraq to bring it under control, and nothing was getting better. Iraq represented a good, high-paying job for military veterans with the right skills, but came with some hellish risks.

The road from Baghdad Airport to downtown was a constant danger to military traffic and security contractors. Explosive devices were set on the road almost every night, and sometimes in daylight. The devices were endlessly creative, but all relied on a fuse of some type, explosive charge and a power source – a battery. Some were designed to explode on contact and others were detonated by an individual nearby with a transmitter. That individual could even be in a car. The most damaging IEDs to soldiers on foot were filled with rocks, nails or other fragments to cause gruesome wounds. IEDs were causing most of the American casualties now in Iraq.

Ashford was just a few feet from the gas can when he saw the Toyota Corolla coming toward their position at high speed, headlights off, weapons dangling from the open windows.

He crouched in firing position, took aim, and then everything went white.

When he awoke, he was aware of several people standing over him. He could feel nothing and had no hearing, and could not make out their words. He drifted in and out of consciousness, at some point aware he was on a stretcher being loaded into the cargo bay of a large transport aircraft.

His next awareness was of a U.S. military hospital in Germany, and in the coming days he learned he had lost both legs and nearly bled to death on the highway in Baghdad. He would not be going back. He would face months of recuperation, follow-up surgeries and physical therapy, and would be fitted with prosthetic legs, and sent back to the states. To what?

"You're very lucky to be alive," his nurse said.

"Am I?" he asked.

One of his paramilitary colleagues from the ambush stopped to visit him in Germany, en route home on leave.

"'What happened to the guys who got me?" the legless man asked.

"We sprayed the car with fire, killed the driver and captured the others – just kids maybe twenty years old," the other man said. "Lined them up and sent them to be with Allah on the spot."

DAN PEDERSEN

Chesterfield Man

Ryan Ashford's motorized wheelchair whined as he drove it out to the mailbox. It was a sunny morning and he had the road to himself, living in the only house at the end of a half-mile lane in the woods near Greenbank. On the way out and back, he'd have time to smoke a Chesterfield.

The house was a double-wide modular with arched windows in the living room, which faced the shipping lanes of Puget Sound – pleasant enough for a seventy-three-year-old disabled veteran and former mercenary. But the explosion that had taken his legs below the knees had destroyed his will to live. For a soldier of fortune, this felt like the bitter end.

He broke into a fit of coughing – he still smoked. The cigarettes hadn't killed him, but a terrorist he never saw nearly did, with an improvised explosive device. Just some kid.

Since the explosion seven years ago, Ashford had all but given up. When he looked in the mirror, he saw a pitted, leathery face, a long scar running down his cheek, and a haystack of gray hair. A full beard mostly covered his disfigured jaw.

He pulled a .45 caliber revolver from his shoulder holster, held it up in front of him and spun the barrel. He put it to his temple for a moment, then slipped the weapon back into the holster. It was a routine he rehearsed every so often.

Ashford liked the .45 because it fired a larger round with more knock-down power than some of the popular alternatives. He liked knowing it was there and he could pull the trigger if things got too bad – the end of pain once and for all.

A young home health worker came once a week and helped him bathe. He took off his prosthetic legs and sat naked for her on a chair in his shower. As she ran a soapy washcloth over his shoulders, he undressed her with his eyes, but there would be no more women for him. They looked at him now with pity and shock.

Infections of the wound sites on his legs were frequent, sending him to the hospital in Mount Vernon for days at a time. He'd been hospitalized several times, too, for pneumonia, his lungs weakened by a lifetime of smoking. His social life consisted of weekly trips to the pain center in Oak Harbor.

Ashford's doctor wanted to cut higher on his legs, to remove the putrified, infected areas. "You're not cutting any more off me," Ashford said. "Find some other way."

On his last trip to the hospital, he found himself sharing a room with another patient.

"What are you in for?" he shouted through the curtain to the unseen patient in the next bed.

"Cancer," was the answer.

"How bad is it?"

"Pretty bad. How about you?"

"Lost my legs. Now I've got some damn infection. Are you going to live or die?"

"I'm not sure. Eventually we all die."

"That's what I'm thinking, too," Ashford said. "I don't want to die, but I don't want to live, either."

Ashford hadn't intended to come back to Whidbey Island after the Langston job here in 2008. It left him feeling vulnerable, even moreso because someone knew about Christy Morris and was in a position to disclose that to the police, also.

Common sense told him to stay as far away as possible. He had done several tours in Iraq and Afghanistan, continuing to sign up even after he was really too old for it. But then after the explosion, he had to find somewhere to wait to die. The island was home, to the extent that he had one anywhere. His parents had both died ten years ago and he had no siblings. He was just hiding out here, anyway.

Ashford's cell phone rang, and he stopped the chair to answer it.

"How are you doing?" the caller asked.

"'Bout the same."

"Is there anything I can do for you?"

"Give me back my legs."

Ashford often thought about the two civilians he had killed in the gravel pit, years ago. They had died quickly and painlessly. Maybe he was paying for that, and Christy Morris, with the slow death he'd been suffering since the bomb went off.

"Listen," the caller said. "There's a little investigation brewing in the old Langston case."

"So I read in the paper."

"It won't go anywhere. It's just a young deputy trying to make a name for herself, but she has no idea what she's stuck her nose into."

"She had better not," he said, but the truth was he really didn't care anymore. His life was over.

"Do you know where Delaney is?"

"No idea. Probably long since dead in the jungle."

"Probably so. Don't worry. I'm on top of this."

The truth was, Ashford did know where Delaney was. But the two friends had always protected each other by compartmentalizing. Information like that was strictly on a need-to-know basis.

The caller hung up and dialed another number.

"Marvin, I need you to take care of something right away," the caller said. "That deputy is snooping around and we've got a loose end."

It was the call Trammel had expected for some time, and dreaded. He had a good life with a wife and grandchildren. He wanted to put the past behind him.

"It needs to look like suicide. Just one thing," the caller said. "He packs a forty-five and you'll need to get that away from him."

Kat found the turn to Ashford's driveway and followed the narrow lane from the mailbox out to his home on a bluff overlooking Puget Sound. The gravel was weedy and it looked like not many cars came this way. When she pulled within view of his double-wide, she noted it was pleasant enough, nondescript. She wondered what help he could give her all these years after the murders, well aware that despite his politics at the time, he probably had nothing to do with them.

She parked, got out and let *Duncan* out to snoop around. She couldn't take her eye off the GM Hummer in the driveway. She'd never been this close to one before and walked over to look inside. What kind of person needed a car like this? It had all the classic military touches, but something about it was odd. There were no floor pedals but a special set of hand controls. This vehicle had been modified for use by a disabled driver.

She turned, walked over to the house, stepped up on the porch and knocked.

No answer.

"Mr. Ashford," she called. "Sheriff's department, Mr. Ashford. Is anyone home?"

She waited and heard no sounds from inside. She pounded harder. After a moment she stepped off the porch and went looking for *Duncan*, who had disappeared around the front of the house on the water side.

Duncan was standing at the edge of the bluff, sniffing and staring at the entrance of a trail that zigzagged down to the beach, maybe a hundred feet below. No doubt he was visualizing some animal that had passed that way during the night. Deputies usually didn't look around someone's property without reasonable cause or permission, but if Ashford showed up and challenged her, she could always say she was looking for her dog, who had given her the slip.

In fact, *Duncan* had seen something below. The view on this side was breathtaking and Kat took a moment to register what his posture was telling her. When she looked at the rocky beach below, a sick feeling came over her.

At the base of the cliff, in the rocks, was a pile of debris and something fleshy that looked like part of a human body.

"*Duncan,* we'd better get down there," she said, starting down the trail at a fast walk. Before she even reached the spot, she could see the tangled remains of a motorized wheelchair and two prosthetic legs at the water's edge. She could just make out a dark pool near his head that must be blood, and she assumed he had struck a large boulder. She was breathing hard now. He was obviously dead but she had to confirm it.

Reaching the body, she checked his carotid artery for a pulse and clicked the transmit button on her shoulder radio.

"Kat Brown. I have a deceased male on the beach at Greenbank – possible accident or suicide. Hang on a sec," she said, digging for the wallet in his pants pocket. "It's the homeowner, Ryan Ashford. I'm going to need the coroner and some backup to secure the scene."

"This is Shane," came the reply. "I'm on my way. Twenty minutes."

There was a burst of static on Kat's radio. "Coroner notified," the dispatch operator said. "About an hour out. Backup en route."

Two other officers arrived and found their way down to the beach. Kat left them to watch over the body and gather the mangled wreckage of the chair while she returned to the house.

She had just reached the top of the bluff and was rounding up *Duncan* when Shane's car came up the road. She hurried over to her own vehicle.

"Hop in," she said to *Duncan*, indicating the front seat of her cruiser, and he did.

Shane parked, got out and looked at Kat. "Is that *Duncan* making calls with you?"

"What? Oh, yeah. Just giving him a little break from home."

Kat could see a comment forming on Shane's lips but no words came. She decided to head it off.

"What do you make of this whole situation?" she asked.

"The coincidence is striking. It could be suicide. That wouldn't be surprising for someone who'd lost his legs. But with the investigation reopened, you have to wonder about the timing."

"That's what I think, too," Kat said. "If he knew anything about Elliott Langston, his lips are sealed now."

"Where do you think he went over the edge?" Shane asked.

Kat led him to the spot Duncan had found where the blufftop vegetation was sparse. "It wouldn't take much to drive or push a wheelchair right through this thin spot," she said. They looked for skid marks and found none, though the grass was compressed in two ruts about the width of the chair's fat tires.

Something in the grass caught her eye, and Kat reached down and picked up the butt of a cigarette. Right next to the filter was the word "Chesterfield."

Kat and Shane spent the next hour going through Ashford's house and car, checking drawers and glove box, looking for a suicide note they did not find, and any other clues to the life of this former special forces soldier who had been prominent in Marlene Meyers's political movement.

To Kat's pleasant surprise, Ashford's laptop was not password-protected. She opened his email and started to scan. Aside from a few contacts who appeared to be military or ex-military, he didn't have many friends. But an outbound email to a Dennis Delaney caught her eye. It had been sent just hours earlier and was titled, "Snooping."

"Better lie low for a while," Ashford had written. "Sheriff is snooping and The Boss is nervous. You and I are expendable."

Kat unplugged the computer and carried it to her car.

"What have you got there?" Shane asked.

"Another lead – another possible conspirator."

While they were talking, coroner Ralph Emerson emerged from the beach trail, followed by the two deputies carrying a stretcher with Ashford's body on it. Without legs, it wasn't that big or heavy. They set it down next to the doctor's vehicle, and one of the deputies came over.

"We're going to get a little landing craft from Port Townsend for the chair. It's too heavy to drag the wreckage up the trail," he said. "Must be three-hundred-fifty pounds, one of the big ones."

"I thought you'd want this," he added. It was Ashford's cell phone. "I found it about thirty feet from the body."

"I sure do."

"He was wearing a holster on his belt but it was empty. We looked all over for the gun but didn't find it. Didn't want kids to come across it, walking the beach."

"You're sure you looked thoroughly?"

"Very much so."

Kat thought it odd there was no gun. She and

Shane hadn't found one in the house, either, though they'd found a box of forty-five caliber shells in the kitchen cupboard. She would check to see what was registered to him.

Trammel hadn't intended to keep the gun. He had grabbed it away from Ashford while he lit a cigarette. Ashford had been sitting on the porch in his chair when Trammel drove up. Trammel simply walked up on the porch, said "Good afternoon," and made a quick move for the gun. It happened so fast Ashford never had a chance to react.

"Wow, Marvin, I didn't know you had a move like that in you," Ashford said. "I always knew these smokes would kill me," he laughed, "but not this way. Who sent you? I never knew who hired us."

Trammel ignored the question. "Let's go for a walk out back," Trammel said.

"You walk. I'll ride."

Trammel supposed Ashford knew what was coming next. He'd done this enough times to other people in his years as a mercenary. Trammel wondered how it must feel to be on the losing end in a moment like this, the one who was suddenly powerless.

"We had some good times back in the day," Ashford said, making conversation. "The four of us were quite a team."

"That was a long time ago," Trammel said. "Life goes on. Some of us still have a lot to lose."

"Mind if I finish my cigarette?" Ashford asked.

"Be quick."

Ashford was buying a little time, no doubt reviewing whether he had any options.

When the cigarette burned down to a stub, Trammel declared, "I think that's about it, Ryan, and waved him to the edge. Trammel thought Ashford seemed oddly resigned. "You're doing me a favor," were Ashford's last words as he gunned the chair. Trammel watched the chair pitch forward and tumble end-over-end till it crashed on the rocks below, and Ashford's body went flying.

Then he turned and hurried back to his car. He didn't realize he still had the gun till he got home. He got a shovel, walked out to the compost pile and dug a hole, and buried it there. Then he dialed a number, got an answering machine, and said simply, "It's done." He was still shaking.

Back at the office, Kat was on the phone to the tech people at the county. She'd gone back and found a few emails Delaney had sent Ashford. By a lucky break, his internet service provider was a private company in The Dalles, Oregon. It was a small town of about fifteen thousand in a county of just twenty-seven thousand. She had a good, fighting chance of finding Delaney.

At Kat's request, the sheriff still had not released the name of the second victim in the case, Patty Gibbs. Walter Gibbs remained a suspect behind the murders. He might or might not know his own sister was one of the victims. Kat hoped to tie him to the murders or clear his name before springing Patty's identity on him.

Meanwhile, a search of Wasco County property records turned up several Delaneys but just one Dennis Delaney, who owned a farm outside Dufur, on the north-south highway east of the Cascade Range. She found several articles about him by searching the local newspaper and ag websites. A local ag association webpage gave an email address that coincided with the one in Ashford's computer.

Delaney was a prominent conservative, and president of the local agricultural association. He was married and apparently had left his para-military career and moved to Oregon to take up farming. He grew an eclectic variety of crops including grass seed, some wine grapes and industrial hemp. Ashford's connection to Delaney was not clear, but Ashford had sent a warning to him about the renewed sheriff's investigation. That was a huge red flag. Were there two killers? Like Ashford, Delaney had been a military contractor and a government employee, though the nature of his government service was not clear.

While Ashford's death could easily be explained as suicide, its timing invited deeper investigation, as did the missing gun. Coincidences were piling up. Kat found Delaney's phone number within just a few minutes online and dialed. On the third ring, a woman with a Spanish accent answered. "Oh yes, he's right here," she said. "Let me put him on the line to you."

"Mr. Delaney," Kat began, "it's Kat Brown with the Island County Sheriff on Whidbey Island. How are you today? I'm calling about a friend of yours, Ryan Ashford."

Delaney hesitated and Kat sensed he was confused, not quite sure how to respond. "What's this about? What makes you say he's a friend?"

"He's been emailing you, for one thing."

The silence on the line told Kat she had caught him completely off guard.

"Oh that. We're just a couple of old military buddies. Quite a few of us keep in touch."

"I'm looking into a cold case, a couple of murders, from 2008. Mr. Ashford wrote to you about it and said, quote, to 'lie low because we're expendable.'"

"Oh geez, I don't know what he was talking about. Ever since he was injured by an IED and lost his legs, his mind has been all over the place. I think he's depressed and delusional."

The remark was pathetic and desperate. He was thinking on the fly, and not very well. He didn't realize how much Kat knew, but she was sure she had shaken him.

"Did you know I found him dead yesterday? He

apparently ran his wheelchair off a cliff, but whether it was suicide or homicide, we're still working on that."

Kat heard a groan, and nothing more.

She continued. "If you know anything about the events of 2008, I sure hope you'll help us out."

"That was a long time ago," he remarked. "Lots of water under the bridge since then."

"Not so terribly long. Two people died. And now Ryan Ashford. And from what I see, I think your life could be in danger. We're going to solve this case, and if you help us, we can help you, too. And it might go better for you."

Silence.

"Write down my number," Kat said, reading it slowly and repeating it twice. "Thank you for your time." She ended the call.

Kat was aware she'd given Delaney reason to run, but really didn't think he would. He was a farmer, married, and an established member of the community. If he ran, he'd lose everything he had built. She was counting on him to think about what she'd said very carefully and cut a deal.

If Ward had removed Ashford as a witness, was it possible he would come for him, as well? It seemed unthinkable. How much had Ashford said before he died?

Delaney hung up the phone and glanced over at his wife, who had been unloading the dishwasher but stopped during the call. She was drying her hands with a dishtowel now, and watching him, waiting for him to speak. From the concern on her face, he knew she could tell this call had shaken him.

"Is it bad news?" she asked.

"Bad enough. It's some things I did in my past that I thought were settled. I need to do some thinking."

Of course, those matters had never been settled.

He thought about both events often, with regret and sadness. In the years since the Langston murders, so much had changed in the world. He now wondered if he'd had it exactly backwards. What if Elliott Langston had been on the right side all along, and he and Ashford had been working for the wrong side? Over the years, Delaney had done some bad things, but always as an agent of the U.S. government. This was different. At the time of the murders, with the hubris of youth, he and Ryan Ashford thought they were doing the right thing, the patriotic thing.

Delaney looked at his wife and smiled weakly. He could still see the dark-haired beauty whose bright spirit and intelligence had won his heart in that jungle camp. She was the steady one, the practical one, who tackled problems one step at a time. The prospect of losing her and the good life they had built here was more than he could bear.

God and Country

"This is war!" Marlene Meyers shouted from speakers positioned all around the sports stadium. "We're in a war for God and country, and unless we all stand up and fight right now, we can kiss our Christian nation goodbye. Democracy has failed!"

The football field in front of Marlene was packed with people, and still more filled the lower bleachers. Marlene was standing on a platform in the center of the field.

"Mar-lene, Mar-lene, Mar-lene!" the crowd chanted.

Kat was watching a video clip on Meyers's website – "Marlene Meyers for Senate."

"Godless liberals, socialists, queers and immigrants have stolen and squandered the American Dream. I'm tired of giving handouts from my hard-earned tax dollars to the dregs of society who are too lazy to work. Stand with me and we're going to take it back."

Marlene, in military-style khakis and a black beret, was wearing a gun on her hip as she waved her hands for emphasis. This was unreal – she was dressed like a guerilla soldier. In her right hand she held a Bible. Kat couldn't believe her eyes. Marlene's long, blonde hair flowed with the breeze in the heat of a California afternoon, and behind her was the U.S.

flag and half-a-dozen black and red Meyers flags. She was telegenic and mesmerizing, even in her seventies, and surrounded herself with all the right props. She had movie-star good looks.

The camera panned the crowd and Kat saw a sea of white faces, many of them older men waving Meyers flags and Christian crosses. Someone held aloft a placard saying, "Jesus is coming." Someone else carried a Confederate flag. One was carrying a noose. Another waved a sign, 'String Him Up,' apparently a reference to the state governor. What in the world did these people stand for?

"Thank you, good people, for coming out today," Marlene said.

Kat couldn't tell whether Marlene planned to run for election or just to storm the capitol and take the office by force. Why settle for senate?

Around the base of the platform, facing the audience, stood Marlene's bodyguard of leather-clad men with their motorcycles. Some bore Nazi Swastikas or flew Confederate flags from their machines. Others wore helmets and body armor. They looked to be itching for a fight.

This was a rough crowd, and Marlene was stoking their fear and anger masterfully. Kat hadn't heard Marlene outline any policy proposals or statements of principle, just sound bites that would play well on YouTube, Instagram, Twitter and Facebook. The video made her shiver. She could well imagine how Marlene's stint as county commissioner could have inspired zealous followers to commit violence, even murder.

Kat could sense that Shane Lindstrom had come up behind her and was watching the video over her shoulder. When she turned to acknowledge him, he shook his head and turned away. "You've got a tiger by the tail this time," he said to her. "If Marlene was behind the Langston murders, and we go after her, it's going to stir up a hornet's nest with her followers."

"I know," Kat said. "I was hoping we weren't going there."

Kat was pretty sure Ashford and Delaney had pulled the trigger on Elliott Langston. But was that as high as it went? Ashford's death suggested someone else was orchestrating what happened.

Had the two soldiers also transported the bodies to the hole in the street? Kat didn't think so. They were paramilitaries. As far as she knew, neither one had a dump truck. This argued that a driver, likely in the gravel business, also was involved – a third member of the conspiracy.

The Oak Harbor conservative, Larry Ward, could easily have his fingers in a plot to murder Langston. So could Marvin Trammel. Ma Barker had plenty of reason to want Langston gone, and she had the heavy equipment for it, but didn't seem like the murdering type, and she'd been romantically involved with him. Kat had to admit she rather liked Ma, who came across as guileless and refreshing.

Walter Gibbs and Marlene Meyers remained Kat's top suspects, but she wasn't quite ready to lay her cards on the table.

FINAL COVER-UP

Who Do You Trust?

Elliott Langston's disappearance in 2008 had removed the biggest county-permitting obstacle of all for Walter Gibbs. He knew he would be a suspect if only because he had so much to gain. Now, with the renewed sheriff's investigation, he felt the pressure once more. For years this had been a forgotten case.

The deputy who'd visited him had asked about subcontractors with a gravel truck who might have had access to the street project, who could have delivered the bodies under cover of darkness. He'd gone over the list repeatedly, and it was making him question his ability to judge people.

In his heart, he was convinced suspicions would flow toward Marlene Meyers, the biggest investor in his Gibbs Addition housing development, but she wasn't in the gravel business. She had left the island after losing her bid for reelection, but remained heavily invested in Gibbs Addition and other development projects.

The sheriff had not released the name of the other victim whose skeleton was found next to Langston's. Gibbs wondered whether the person had ever been identified, or whether the sheriff was withholding that information for some reason. The mystery of those cold case murders was growing, and he suspected the cold cases weren't anywhere near as cold as they'd been just a week earlier.

On a whim, he dialed a friend on the county commission.

"I'm just curious," he said. "The sheriff hasn't released the identity of the second victim in the Langston case. Do you happen to know if they've been identified?"

"It's sensitive information," the commissioner said. "I'm not free to share it."

"I'm not asking who it is – just whether they've been identified," Gibbs said.

"They have. That's all I can say, and you didn't hear it from me."

Kat had reached the point where she needed to make something happen. She knew Ashford and Delaney were connected by their service as private security contractors and wondered if they were also connected to others whose names had come to her attention. Working from Ashford's birth year, and the assumption he might have grown up on the island, she went back and looked at local high school yearbooks online.

Bingo!

On page sixty-four of the nineteen-sixty-five Oak Harbor annual, there was a crewcut Ashford in a wrestling singlet. In the same photo, she found Delaney, Trammel and Ward. Holy cow! All had wrestled on the same squad, for the same school, in the same year.

Homecoming queen that year was a bombshell blonde named Marlene Meyers, "most likely to succeed." It was beginning to look like whatever had happened to Elliott Langston had started with a group of high school students more than fifty years ago.

A search of vital statistics showed that Ashford had been married to a Louise Ashford, nee Kristoferson, and they divorced in nineteen-ninety-eight. She was a sophomore in the nineteen-sixty-seven annual, active in pep club.

Kat traced Kristoferson to Stanwood, actually Camano Island, where she was now married again and living as Louise Moeller. Camano Island was part of Island County. Maybe it was time for a drive.

"I'm headed over to Camano Island for an interview on the Langston case," Kat told Shane. "I've found Ashford's ex-wife."

She considered calling ahead to make sure Louise Moeller was home, but often found it more effective to just show up and surprise her subjects. She swung home, picked up *Duncan,* and headed for the state ferry terminal at Clinton, a faster and shorter way to Camano than driving the length of the island and crossing Deception Pass Bridge to Fidalgo Island and Skagit Valley up north.

"Nice day for a boat ride, eh, *Duncan?*" Kat asked as *Duncan* hung his head out the passenger window and inhaled the marine air.

Kat didn't get many opportunities to visit Camano Island. There was a friendly rivalry between the two halves of Island County, with Camano Islanders joking that their nice weather was because Whidbey served as a barrier to storms – Breakwater Island, they called it.

Kat's favorite shortcut to Camano was to exit Intestate Five at Arlington and head cross-country through Silvana, a small farming community in the hinterlands. The Stillaguamish River runs through this community and the railway that once transported farm crops runs through the center of town. One of the local icons was a classic old church from the 1800s overlooking the valley – "the Little White Church on the Hill." Pioneer families, Scandinavians like Shane Lindstrom, built Silvana Lutheran in 1890 and services were still held there. Kat liked rural places like this, where there are still reminders of the past.

On this summer afternoon the farm fields were lush green. The aroma of dairy manure hung in the air, but it wasn't unpleasant. *Duncan,* mouth open, eyes closed and tongue out, clearly thought the dairy air was wonderful. Something about a happy dog makes the whole day worthwhile.

At Stanwood, Kat crossed the narrow slough that separates Camano Island from the mainland. Unlike Whidbey Island, Camano was more of a bedroom community with no real commercial centers. The locals did most of their shopping just across the bridge in Stanwood. As on Whidbey, the north end was more built up and prosperous; the south was more forested and wild. Kat knew the island had several especially lovely parks for camping and fishing.

Shane was an amateur historian and had told her that in the centuries before white contact, when canoes were the principal transportation, the two islands had been closely joined. Water remained the "highway system" in the steamboat era of the late 1800s and early 1900s. Island County was the product of a time when water transportation was dominant. Roads were little more than primitive trails.

Ironically, the development of roads and bridges actually pushed the two islands apart, necessitating many miles of driving to get from one to the other. Even though the main county courthouse was still located in Coupeville on Whidbey Island, geography made it necessary for Camano to have a county administration building where they could receive many of the same services closer to home, including a sheriff's substation. Many Whidbey Islanders had never set foot on Camano, which they could see from their living rooms just a few miles across Saratoga Passage.

The drive to Camano took Kat from Island County to Snohomish County, and then back into Island county. Once she reentered Island County on the bridge at Stanwood, it took her twenty minutes more on picturesque country roads to reach Madrona Beach, on the island's west side, and the Moeller home overlooking Saratoga Passage.

She parked behind a red Ford Explorer and got out. She took a moment to watch all the activity at a bird feeder and birdbath that was bubbling water in the front yard – goldfinches, chickadees and a whole family of nuthatches. Then she walked up to the door and knocked. A moment later, the door opened and Kat was looking at a white-haired woman in her seventies. Behind her stood a distinguished gentleman in a bolo tie and khaki slacks, holding a deck of cards.

"Louise Moeller?" Kat asked.

"Yes."

Kat introduced herself, and Louise invited her in and showed her to a place at the table with a view of the water. The gentleman was her husband, Paul, who had been about to start a game of Bridge. He excused himself so the two women could talk.

"Were you once married to a Ryan Ashford?" Kat asked.

"Yes, more than twenty years ago."

"I'm sorry to say he died this week."

Louise gasped. "I had no idea. Had his legs become infected again?"

"We don't know all the particulars yet. We found his body and wheelchair at the base of the bluff in front of his house."

Louise was silent a moment. "He had a hard life and I don't think the last few years were very good for him, from what little I heard. We had very little to do with each other."

Kat let the comment sit a moment.

"I assume it's suicide?" Louise asked.

"We're not one hundred percent sure yet. We're investigating the circumstances – whether he took his own life or might have been pushed."

Louise nodded. "The way he lived, anything is possible."

"I wanted to go back ask you about an earlier time – 2008. Can you remember what was going on in his life then?"

"Oh gosh, it's been a long time. We'd been essentially separated for years, still married but leading mostly separate lives. The years run together."

"It would have been when Marlene Meyers was a county commissioner," Kat said, "if that jogs your memory at all."

"Oh heavens, her!" Louise exclaimed. "He was enamored with her – all the boys were. She was in his graduating class in high school, you know."

"Yes, I recently discovered that."

"I always felt I was in competition with Marlene Meyers for Ryan, but Larry Ward cut him off by making the first move. Marlene and Larry were quite an item in high school."

"How did that end?" Kat asked.

"I'm not sure it ever really did," Louise said. "After graduation they were both very political, as was Ryan. The boys went into the military. Marlene went into politics and lobbying."

"So your husband was fairly politicized?"

"Very! But the word I'd use is radicalized. That became one of the issues between us. In high school he seemed very all-American, but as the years passed, he changed and became quite hardened, consumed with hatred toward people he considered lefties or racially inferior, whose views didn't line up with his. In high school he was a handsome hunk. After he joined the military, he became a skinhead, and I never got used to it. I guess it was just symbolic of what was going on inside him."

"So back to 2008, around Thanksgiving," Kat resumed.

"I remember he was home then, getting ready to

leave for the Middle East on a new contract. We had a small, quiet meal together. But as usual I only had part of his attention. He was hanging out with his buddies on that visit – rather distracted."

"Anything usual about his behavior?" Kat asked.

"He was always distant and secretive. There was one night, just before he left, he said not to wait up for him. I wondered if he was seeing some other woman. He claimed he had something to do that might keep him out late. He was back the next day and never said any more about it. I took him to the airport the next morning and saw him off to the Middle East. I decided right then and there to get a lawyer and file for divorce. I should have done it years sooner."

"Can you remember his better friends from around the time of Marlene Meyers's stint as county commissioner?"

"He and his buddies were very involved in her movement," Louise said. "Some of the wrestling crowd went into the military around the same time as Ryan and ended up later working as private contractors or for the CIA, which paid more."

"Do you remember the names Delaney, Trammel and Ward?"

"Yes, those guys. All of them."

"Was he especially close to any of them?"

"They were all buddies and I would say all somewhat radicalized. If anyone, Dennis Delaney stands out. Ryan and Dennis were always together."

"Hey," Kat asked. "Did Ryan happen to smoke."

She laughed. "Chesterfield," she said. "That was another issue between us. His friends called him The Chesterfield Man."

"Any idea what brought him back to Whidbey Island after he lost his legs?" Kat asked.

"None," Louise said. "I just know it wasn't me. At that point he really had no home."

"Thank you," Kat said. "You've been very helpful."

For the drive back to Whidbey, Kat decided to take the northern route through Skagit County and across Deception Pass Bridge. It was getting toward rush hour now and she knew the ferry at Mukilteo would be backed up with commuters. Besides, she enjoyed seeing some different country – the broad agricultural plain of the Skagit Valley. Her interview with Louise Moeller had been valuable and it helped alleviate her guilt over such a pleasant day of driving. She could use the time to think about the case.

At Stanwood she turned left, toward Mount Vernon, and at Conway she turned left again, crossing onto the Skagit River Delta, Fir Island, formed by the north and south forks of the Skagit River. This was a scenic shortcut to LaConner and to the highway to Anacortes, offering some spectacular views of Mount Baker across the flat farm fields. She knew a farm stand up ahead, Snow Goose Produce, where they served "immodest ice cream cones," and had her heart set on one.

She was just approaching the bridge, her double-scoop raspberry ice cream cone now a memory, when Shane raised her on the radio.

"Marvin Trammel called," he said. "He'd like to talk with you about the Langston case."

"I'm still about an hour north of the office," Kat said. "I can get there by five o'clock if that works for him, or we can schedule it tomorrow. Let me know what he wants to do. Is he bringing a lawyer?"

"I don't know."

"Either way this feels like something we need to get on the record in the office. We should videotape it."

"I think so, too," Shane said.

Trammel arrived at nine the next morning with his legal counsel, a prominent Oak Harbor lawyer who specialized in criminal defense. There was no banter;

both were grim-faced. Trammel had dressed up for the interview in a white shirt and tie, and khaki slacks.

Kat ushered them into the conference room, brought them coffee and water, and they all sat down. Off to the side sat a tripod with a video camera.

"I'd like to make a formal statement," Trammel said.

"And my client would like to discuss terms for a suspended sentence in return for his assistance in your investigation," the lawyer added.

"We can discuss that, but it really depends on what he did and whether he has anything useful to offer," Kat said. She looked back and forth between the lawyer and Trammel.

The door opened and Shane Lindstrom entered the room, carrying a paper cup with the logo of a local coffee house. "Shane is going to observe," Kat said. "It's standard in these situations." Shane smiled and took a seat at the table.

She added, "I'd like to record this," and she pushed a button on the machine in front of her. A green light appeared atop the camera. Kat identified herself for the recording, stated the date and time, and Trammel and the lawyer both gave their names, along with Shane.

"Why don't you start at the beginning?" Kat said.

Trammel looked down at his hands and said, "I transported the bodies to the dump site in Oak Harbor in nineteen-ninety-seven."

"Did you kill them?"

"Oh my god, no," Trammel said. "I had nothing to do with that. I received a phone call instructing me to go to an abandoned quarry site with my truck and load 'something' – the caller said I would know what it was – and deliver it to the construction site at night, in a load of gravel, and forget it ever happened."

"Who called you?" Kat asked.

"The caller never identified himself. The voice was

a little muffled – maybe he was wearing a mask or something around his neck to alter his voice – but I think I know who it was."

Kat and Shane leaned forward and waited.

"Larry Ward. He said 'The Boss' needed this done."

"Who was The Boss?"

"I'm not sure. Honestly, I always wondered if it was Larry himself. I was in the middle of a big job hauling gravel for Gibbs. I did a lot of work for him and others. We all hated Elliott Langston. I recognized his body when I went to pick up the load."

"What about the woman? Did you know who she was?"

"No idea. That really shook me and always has."

"What's your connection to Larry Ward?"

"High school sports. Several of us wrestled together and got pretty involved in politics. We saw what was happening with all the lefties and Communists, and decided to do something about it. So we formed a secret society. We called ourselves The Brothers and pledged to one another that we would act and not just talk."

"So who were the members of this group?" Kat asked.

"Myself, Larry Ward, Ryan Ashford, Dennis Delaney."

"Do you know how Ryan Ashford died?"

"I heard he ran his wheelchair off a cliff."

"Did you have something to do with that?"

Trammel went silent and looked at his lawyer. The lawyer leaned over and whispered in Trammel's ear, and then said, "My client has no comment on that."

"That's too bad, because I'm sitting here trying to decide whether he's being fully cooperative or holding back," Kat replied. "It will make a difference in whatever deal we strike, and what we recommend to the prosecutor.

"It's okay," Trammel said to his lawyer. "Let me explain.

"I got another call the other day from Larry. He said Ashford was depressed and suicidal, and The Boss was worried about him breaking his silence. He wanted me to go to Ashford's house and take care of things."

"Meaning?

"I'm not sure. I was sick about the whole thing. I hoped I could talk to him and settle him down."

"You think Ashford was the trigger man?" Kat asked.

"I'm guessing he was."

"So what did you do after Larry called you?"

"I drove to Ashford's house and couldn't find him. Looked over the edge of the bluff and saw his body and wheelchair on the beach, and I got out of there."

"Ashford was wearing an empty holster when we found him," Kat said. "Do you know anything about the gun?"

Trammel looked confused and shrugged.

*

Walter Gibbs sat back in his chair and closed his eyes. His mind was thousands of miles away, going back in time to when he and Patty were just children. He was pushing his eight-year-old sister as she swinging out over the river on a knotted rope. It was an idyllic memory. She had her feet twisted tightly atop the lowest knot and her arms stretched over her head, hands cupped around the rope as high as she could reach. She was lean and pigtailed, her brown eyes sparkling as she laughed. Even as a child, she had her mother's dark beauty and lustrous black hair.

Patty and the rope came swinging back and she yelled, "Higher. Higher!"

In the dappled shade of the tree canopy, Walter took a few steps forward and pushed as hard as he could with both arms and Patty swung way out over the lazy river, the rope climbing ever higher. It was a classic August afternoon in the Blue Ridge mountains of western North Carolina. Walter could picture the memory as if it were yesterday. At just the right moment, at the height of the arc, Patty released her grip and fell into the cooling waters with a big splash. She swam back in her cutoffs, climbed up on the beach dripping wet, wearing a satisfied grin, and laughed in that sweet voice that was music to him.

"Perfect!" she said. "Now it's your turn."

Walter adored her.

Growing up on an isolated farm in the hill country, Walter and Patty had been each other's best pals and playmates as far back as they could remember. Their parents scratched out a livelihood raising pigs, tobacco, corn and even a few Fraser fir Christmas trees. The trees were their dad's special favorite, prized for their fragrance, shape and needle characteristics that they've been chosen more than any other species for the White House.

"Every crop helps out every other crop," their dad said. "If one of them doesn't do so well, the others fill in." He laughed, "And no matter what, we'll always have a nice Christmas tree."

That was just like his dad, putting much of his land into a crop that took years to grow and harvest. Walter thought his dad was a good man but not a very good farmer. "I could make more doing something else," his dad said, "but I like being my own boss." Walter never saw his parents argue. They worked hard and didn't complain.

None of their farming was on a large enough scale to put them ahead. Their home was a modest wood-frame house, thirty miles from town. Patty and Walter rode the school bus for an hour each way and wore mostly hand-me-down clothing from a local thrift shop. When a hole or tear appeared, their mom patched it. In the evenings they helped their parents with chores -- dishes and laundry, feeding the pigs, filling the firewood bin, spreading hay and wood chips, gathering eggs from the hens.

Walter's least favorite job was on Sundays, helping their dad butcher a chicken. In those days, on the farm, families did their own butchering. There was no going to the supermarket and buying a chicken wrapped in plastic. Walter's dad would walk into the pen with a long-handled hook and slip the hook around the legs of the first plump chicken he could catch.

Holding the poor chicken by the legs, he'd lay it across a stump and bring the axe down on its head. The headless body then often ran a few steps around the yard before the legs stopped kicking reflexively, and the dead chicken fell over. With a pan of hot water, Walter and Patty would pluck off the feathers, and later their mother would fry or roast the chicken for dinner. Walter pictured Patty watching her mother prepare the meal. He knew she'd always admired her mom's beauty, her dark eyes and raven hair. Her mom said she was part Cherokee, and Patty no doubt it was true.

When the chores, dinner and homework were done, Patty and Walter fell into their beds and stole a few moments to dream. Patty wore a headband with an eagle feather and when she got old enough, she wanted to work for the Cherokee Nation. She knew every detail of the Trail of Tears story, where the Cherokee of North Carolina and other Southern states were forcibly removed from their lands to a reservation in Oklahoma.

The native story fascinated her – how the Cherokee people had lived in balance with the land for thousands of years as an advanced and remarkable democratic civilization. Knowing that her mom had Cherokee blood just added to her desire to know more about her people. Patty was not part of any crowd at school and Walter knew she didn't care. She refused to let others define her, but the mocking and bullying got to Walter and he hated himself for it. More than anything he wanted to belong, to be somebody.

"Hey, Patches!" the other boys taunted him. "Walter Patches Gibbs, I'm talking to you! Get a load of those rags!" they said to each other, staring and pointing at him, and doubling over in laughter. "Did your momma make those pants for you?"

Walter just wanted to get away when the time came. "I'm going to move as far away from here as I can," he told Patty, "and make a lot of money, and I'll help you and take care of you. We won't be poor anymore."

Walter stirred and opened his eyes, and sat up in his chair. Things had gone wrong somehow – his dream and his relationship with Patty. He had done well in the real estate business, living in a community with a strong military presence where the government poured money. Patty had turned her back on all of it and moved out to California, and become a Buddhist. He had fallen out with his only sibling and felt the loss deeply. Her disappearance some years ago still filled him with pain. He wondered if he would ever understand.

Dog Day

Kat watched *Duncan* and *Midnight* run. Roger's dog, *Midnight,* was a water-lover and *Duncan* was a herder, so on this summer evening at Double Bluff Beach they divvied up the stick-chasing and snooping by specialty. Sand was flying as *Duncan* dug a hole for something smelly he had found.

This was another of Kat's trademark beach evenings, when the sun was dropping lower in the sky and the day's heat had broken. Roger was sitting at her side.

"I can already see the difference in *Duncan* since you started working with that behaviorist," Roger said. "He seems more confident and settled. He showed no hesitation about greeting *Midnight.* They're playing nicely together."

"He's responding beautifully to Linda's efforts. I can't believe he was so close to being euthanized as an unstable biter."

"It takes time and patience to work with a dog that has problems. Most people won't invest the time."

"I think I've got a good dog now," Kat said. "Guy has stopped objecting to having a dog and is fully on board with him after seeing the change."

"On a different subject, I can't believe how much progress you've made on the case," Roger said. "You're close to putting all the pieces together."

"I think so, too," Kat said. "I can feel it."

"Do you think Trammel was telling the truth?"

"Probably not the whole truth, probably not everything, but I think he was truthful about the big stuff. What I want to know is how high up this goes. Trammel fingered Ward. Was he The Boss or just the middleman for someone else? And whose idea was it to kill Patricia Gibbs? We've been thinking Elliott Langston was the target, but what if the real target was Patricia? Maybe it wasn't coincidence that she was killed the minute she set foot on the island."

"So who's the next domino to fall?" Roger asked.

"I'm thinking Dennis Delaney – working my way up the food chain."

"Will he talk?"

"These guys are in their seventies," Kat said, "and they've got a problem. They aren't the same people they once were – they've moved on and built new lives. They've carried a terrible secret for years. If Delaney pulled the trigger, he'll have to pay a price, but if he can help us find who's really behind these murders, that's who I want. I want The Boss."

Dennis Delaney sat high up on the seat of his green-and-yellow John Deere cabover and looked out across the golden field, half of which was now ready for the bailer. Manuel would come along behind him and do that part. Even in the enclosed cab, with a fan blowing on him, he was ready for a siesta.

The sun was high overhead and he'd made good use of the morning, starting in the cool of the dawn and working till it was really too hot to keep going. Now he was watching a pair of Red-tailed Hawks soar on the updrafts. Nothing gets the birds of prey stirred up like a freshly-mown field with all those dislodged mice and voles. He was feeling like a naked mouse, himself.

He couldn't get the deputy's call out of his mind. Ryan Ashford was dead and had left a trail of email, and the deputy had made the connection to him, and knew of their shared military experience and political background. Sooner or later, she'd identify Delaney as one of two shooters along with Ashford. He had little to trade for a plea bargain but his knowledge of who else was in The Brothers, who might have been behind all this. If he didn't act soon, he might miss his chance to negotiate a lighter sentence and maybe save his farm and his marriage. He needed to talk to Alicia right away.

There was also the dilemma of what to do about Christy Morris. Ryan, the most culpable of the four, was dead. Should Dennis reveal what he knew? They had all left the scene. They were all drinking. They had all participated in disposing of the body.

He swung his right leg over his left and lowered himself down from the tractor, wondering if this was the last time he'd ever look out at his fields and work the land.

Pulling open the screen door from the back porch, Delaney entered the kitchen and waited for the soft whap behind him. He put down his John Deere baseball cap on the counter and gave his wife a kiss.

"Lunch is ready," his wife said, placing a bowl of hearty vegetable soup and a Cesar salad on the table.

"My favorite," Delaney said softly.

He wasn't sure where to begin. What he was about to say might cost him his wife and everything he had worked to build since retiring from the CIA. It was a miracle he had found her in the Cuban community of Miami, with the help of CIA contacts. She had assumed a new identity but left a thin trail, revealing parts of her story to close friends, who were able to help Dennis find her.

Now reunited, Delaney had carried out his long-ago vision of having coffee with her at a sidewalk café, and a few months later they were married. Today, she would learn he was not only a soldier who had done things in war, but a murderer in his own country as well.

"You seem quiet," she said.

"I have something to tell you."

"What have you run over with the tractor now?" she laughed.

"I'm afraid it's a lot worse than that. I did a very bad thing years ago and it has caught up with me. I don't know what it's going to mean for us. I need to come clean with you and also talk to Manuel, because if I go away for a while, he's going to have to hold things together for all of us."

"Many bad things happen in war," Alicia said.

"This wasn't war. And it wasn't even the first. There was something else, earlier."

Alicia's face was grim. "Just tell me," she said. "Was it a woman? Start at the beginning and tell me."

"You know I was part of a political group when I was in school, with several buddies," Dennis said. "We continued when we all went off to the military, and got pretty active a few years ago when pushback got started against the Navy."

"Yes, you've mentioned your friends."

"It's why I ended up with the CIA. All the way back in high school we wanted to make difference – stand for the right things. We did some things, thinking they were for the right reasons, but in hindsight I'm not sure. We were pretty excited because it was all a big secret and we got our orders from higher up, and we were the foot soldiers."

"Who was giving you orders?" she asked

"It was a guy named Larry Ward, one of our high school wrestling teammates, but I think he was just the intermediary for someone else – someone we all called 'The Boss.' We never knew who The Boss was.

We compartmentalized everything for secrecy and deniability in case one of us got caught. The less each of us knew, the better for all."

"So what are you trying to tell me?"

"Ryan Ashford and I both served in the special forces as you know, and later as independent contractors. In fact we both served in the same outfit at one time. We acquired some pretty useful skills. In about 2008, we got the call to eliminate a local activist on Whidbey Island, who was anti-Navy and anti-development, a thorn in the side of everyone who was trying to get something done. We were blackmailed into doing it."

"Are you saying you and Ryan murdered an American citizen?"

"Technically, Ryan pulled the trigger, but yes, I was his accomplice. I stole the van we used, and I was the driver."

"Oh god." Alicia leaned back in her chair and covered her face with both hands, and got very quiet.

"It was even worse than that because when we went to do the job, there was a woman no one expected and we had to make her disappear, too."

"Oh god. You mustn't tell anyone."

"Who was she?"

"I don't know. I've got no choice but to come forward about it. The sheriff's department on the island has reopened the case and is making big progress on it. To have any hope of a plea bargain, I need to tell them what I know right now."

The twin-engine Beech King Air turbo lifted into a cloudless sky from Columbia Gorge Regional Airport at nine the next morning, with Delaney's lawyer at the controls, and Delaney in the co-pilot's seat.

"Keep an eye out for birds and other traffic," the lawyer said.

Alicia Delaney sat behind them in the cabin as

the ground fall away. Delaney already had called ahead and told Kat he was coming to meet with her and bringing his lawyer. It should be an easy hop in good flying weather over the Cascades and then a direct flight to Paine Field near Everett, the nearest airport with plenty of runway for the aircraft. He was looking at the volcanic crater of Mount St. Helens and, in the distance, the commanding peak of Mount Rainier, with other Cascade volcanoes lined up in the distance. If the circumstances had been any different, this would have been a memorable day for a flying adventure.

Delaney and his lawyer had decided on flying as the best way to get there and back in a day. Since Delaney didn't know if he'd be returning to Oregon after meeting with Island County law enforcement, the plane gave his lawyer and Alicia a way to get home after their meeting. It was one hundred forty-four miles, plus a ferryboat ride, and the flight would take just over an hour.

Soon, they were at twenty thousand feet over Interstate Five and Delaney was looking down at cars and trucks, people going about their everyday lives, with everyday concerns.

It was eleven-thirty by the time they landed, parked the aircraft and made connections to the ferry and Freeland, where Kat wanted to conduct the interview. She and Shane had set up the video camera in the interview room once again.

The arriving party introduced themselves and Delaney asked if Alicia could join them in the conference room.

"We don't normally do that," Kat said, "but I don't see why we can't make an exception if she just listens and lets you and your lawyer do the talking." Kat looked at Alicia, who nodded agreement. It was one small concession Kat could make to set the tone for a cordial meeting.

"Are you Latin American?" Kat asked Alicia. "I noticed your accent, which is quite delightful, by the way."

"Nicaraguan," Alicia responded. "That's where I met Dennis. I've been in the estates now for many years."

Everyone took seats at the table – Dennis Delaney, the lawyer, Kat, Shane and Alicia Delaney. Delaney was a very fit man who obviously spent lots of time in the sun on his farm. Kat pushed the button to start the recording. Everyone introduced themselves for the tape.

Kat turned to the lawyer. "I understand your client would like to make a statement," Kat said.

"Yes, that's right. We'd like to explore a plea deal, taking into account assistance my client is prepared to give to the investigation," the lawyer said.

"We are open to that," Kat said, "if you have anything of value for us. Of course it'll be up to the prosecutor, but we will take into account your cooperation."

The lawyer looked at Delaney and nodded.

"I'm here today to confess I was present at the murder of Elliott Langston and a female companion in 2008. Ryan Ashford and I kidnapped them and took them to an abandoned quarry north of Coupeville, where Ryan shot them."

"You were present but you didn't kill them?"

"That's right. It was Ryan Ashford who shot them."

"And how did he do that?"

"He made them kneel, stepped behind them, and shot each of them once in the back of the head."

"Did you know the identity of the woman?"

"No," Delaney said. "We were waiting in Langston's driveway for him to come home, and when we saw the woman with him it was a complete surprise. We had to eliminate her as a witness."

Alicia Delaney was shaking her head.

"So the murders took place at the quarry – I think I know the spot – and then what? How did you dispose of the bodies?"

"We didn't. That was someone else's job and we never knew who they were."

"So someone else was making the assignments?"

"That's right."

"Who was it?"

"Larry Ward."

"Was this whole thing his idea, or do you think he was working for someone else?"

"I always felt it was someone else, that Larry was just the middleman, but I don't know who it was. He talked about someone called The Boss. Ryan and I wondered about it but the whole idea was to compartmentalize, so no one knew all the details."

"I believe your group had a name."

"We did. The Brothers. The name was Larry's suggestion, back in our senior year when we formed the group."

"What did you do with the vehicle in which you transported the victims?"

"It was a stolen van. After we pulled the bodies off to the side of the clearing, we undressed them and threw all their clothes and personal effects into the vehicle. Then we set it on fire at the quarry."

"Wouldn't it have been easier to burn the bodies with the vehicle?"

"We did as we were told."

"The van is still there all these years later," Kat noted.

She shuffled through some papers on the table in front of her and slid a photograph in front of Delaney.

"This is a picture of the wrestling squad from your senior yearbook," she said.

Delaney looked at it and smiled.

"A long time ago," he said.

"Who's that in the picture with you? Is that Marvin Trammel?"

"It is."

"Do you suppose he had a role in transporting the bodies – I mean, since he had a gravel truck and was part of this group called The Brothers?"

"It's certainly possible. Larry thought he was weak. It would be like Larry to draw Marvin into things, get him to be part of the crime against his neighbor, to make sure he'd keep his mouth shut if anyone came snooping around."

Kat sat there without comment.

"There's something else, too," Delaney said. "We were all blackmailed into doing it by someone who found out the four of us were responsible for the death of a classmate in high school."

"Who was that?" Kat asked.

"A girl named Christy Morris. That case was never solved. It was a hit-and-run accident on West Beach Road. We put the body in the trunk of Ryan's car and buried it on the beach."

Kat leaned back in her chair and looked at Shane, and then back at Delaney.

"Mr. Delaney, would you excuse us for just a moment?" Kat and Shane slid back in their chairs, got up and walked out of the room.

They returned a moment later. "Mr. Delaney, in light of what you've said that you were an accessory to murder, and also to a fatal hit-and-run, we're going to have to arrest and charge you, and hold you here while we talk to the prosecutor."

"My client is not a flight risk," the lawyer said.

"We'll try to work something out if we can," Kat said. "We just need a little time."

DAN PEDERSEN

Perspective

Marlene and Larry sat at a window table at Wakatsuchi Lodge in Sequoia National Park. It was an off-hour, a Tuesday in April, and only one other table of diners were having lunch. The sun was shining from a blue sky, and the view outside the window was of mountains and sequoias. As a prominent public figure, Marlene always wore a red wig and dark glasses for these meetings to disguise her identity.

For decades they had been meeting once or twice a year in places like this – on the Oregon Coast, the wilds of Idaho, or the wine country of Napa Valley.

Larry had reluctantly used a credit card in his own name to register for the night. It would be traceable if the sheriff's department looked at his statements, though there was no record of Marlene's name. In a worst-case scenario, he could say he was working as a campaign consultant for her.

It had taken Larry only about two hours to get to Fresno from Everett's Paine Field on a direct commercial flight. Marlene had met him at Fresno and they'd driven south to Visalia and then up into the foothills at Three Rivers. Larry loved this time of year when whole hillsides of California Golden Poppies were carpeted in orange. The creeks they passed on their drive were running high with snowmelt.

On the way up they had stopped at The General

Sherman Sequoia. Marlene insisted he should see it, estimated to be about 2,300 to 2,700 years old. It had already been an old tree when the United States broke away from England. In that context, it seemed like his life had passed in a heartbeat. Twelve years was nothing, since the murders.

"This may be the last time we can meet like this," Larry said. "The deputy who's investigating the Langston case is closing in on me.

"Dennis and Marvin are trying to figure out who revealed what we did to Christy, and to whom. I never told them it was me. It ended up serving a purpose."

"We go back a long time," Marlene said. "I'll do everything I can to help you if this whole thing blows up."

"I know you will," he said. "And you know that I'll never say anything."

Change

Kat watched a sailboat tack with the afternoon breeze in Holmes Harbor. She was fighting to stay awake. The view from Shane and Elizabeth's deck at the Eagles' Inn B&B was one of the most relaxing she'd found anywhere on the island, and Saturday was her day to kick back and share a glass of wine with friends. Guy was collecting sediment samples from a beach on north Whidbey and *Duncan* was curled up at Kat's feet, sleeping with one eye open. The three friends were sitting in Adirondack chairs, watching swallows hover and swoop as they snatched insects from the air, but Kat's thoughts were still on her case.

"One of the unsettling aspects of digging into an old case like this is that everyone has changed and moved on," she said. "Nothing is the same as it was years ago. The times have changed. The world has changed."

"Well, that's true," Shane said, "except for Elliott Langston and Patricia Gibbs, and Christy Morris. Everything is the same for them. Time stopped and nothing has changed since."

"What's your impression of Dennis Delaney?" Kat asked Shane at last. She ducked as a Rufous Hummingbird shot past her head on its way to a feeder hanging from the eave.

"Are we on a flyway here?" she asked.

"Yes, they cut across the porch," Elizabeth said. "There' a bit obsessed."

"Delaney seems forthcoming," Shane said. "From what we've seen of the suspects in this case, I'd say he has probably done more than any of the others to move on and make a new life for himself."

"That's what I think, too," Kat said. "I find him likeable and somewhat sympathetic. But he participated in the murder of two people and that's hard to just walk away from."

"As a high school kid and a sports hero, things probably seemed pretty clear and straightforward to him – the world was divided between good and bad," Shane said. "Like a lot of idealistic young people – like you and me – he wanted to be on the side of the good guys. Later, after he'd been to war and seen what happens on both sides, no doubt he became disillusioned that everything was so murky."

"He wasn't so very different from Elliott and Patty. They were looking for truth, too, but coming up with different answers," Kat remarked.

Shane nodded. "Did you hear the story of how Delaney met his wife, Alicia?" Shane asked. "His lawyer filled me in when we had a few minutes to talk in the hallway."

Shane explained that Alicia had been an informant for the CIA. The Sandinistas suspected her father of being a government agent and executed her entire family – mother, father, brothers and sisters. She was in peril of the same fate. Both sides in that war were committing atrocities.

He added that Delaney was leading a team of Nicaraguans carrying out sabotage and political retaliation. His team rescued Alicia from the village where she was working as a health aide and then he violated his orders and took a personal risk in putting her on a CIA flight back to the United States. She changed identity and disappeared into the Cuban community of Miami, but he later found her and married her.

"No doubt he saved her life," Shane said, "and maybe this has something to do with her decision to stand by him in the current situation."

"So, are we saying a murderer can change and redeem himself by good works over the course of his life?" Kat asked.

"Now, that is the question. Some people do change," Shane said. "You did."

He had a point. Kat had been headed for a life of burglary and trouble with the law, almost certainly more and more serious crime that would lead to time in the prison system, which would harden her. It was inevitable that, at some point, she would find herself cornered and do something desperate. Would she use a gun if she had it?

Shane and his friends had given her a chance to turn things around. She'd never answered for some of the things she had done. She'd never had to give a full accounting. On the other hand, she'd never done anything as serious as Dennis Delaney – not even close.

Ryan Ashford was dead. Kat wondered if he'd ever felt any remorse about the accident that killed Christy Morris, or murdering Langston. It seemed apparent that Marvin Trammel had not – he was just trying to weasel his way out of accountability. Then there was Larry Ward, the mastermind of this group. He seemed the least changed and least remorseful of them all – still a true believer in what they had set out to do all those years ago. Was he the link to someone higher up. If so, who?

The Food Chain

Kat parked her car by the flagpole in Larry Ward's front yard. She and Shane walked to the door and knocked.

After a moment, Ward opened it.

"You again."

"Turn around please and place your hands behind your back," she said. "I am arresting you for the murders of Elliott Langston and Patricia Gibbs in 2008."

Without resistance, Ward did as he was told.

"This is just ridiculous," he said. "Based on what?"

"Based on the testimony of three witnesses." Kat led him to the car, opened the back door, placed her hand on his head and guided him into the back seat.

"I suggest you call a lawyer and think about how you can help us, because right now you're the fall guy for someone we both know really called the shots."

She booked him into the jail, dropped Shane at the office, and announced she was clocking out for an hour. She swung home and picked up *Duncan,* and drove to Freeland Park, where she could walk him and do some thinking. The investigation had reached a turning point and the next step would be big.

Everyone had some pain or need in their life –

some disappointment from childhood, an injustice they believed was done to them, a sense that they needed to prove something to a parent or others, or to compensate for a sense of powerlessness. Kat knew this was true of Larry Ward, whose father pushed him to excel in everything. In her studies at Boise State University, they'd discussed that most people spend their whole lives trying to validate the image they have of themselves. *I'm a fighter, an underdog, a patriot, a nice person, an airhead or a drunk.* The details didn't matter but the need to validate was true of everyone.

This had been the case with Ward, Ashford, Delaney and Trammel. They had grown up in a community with a strong military identity and saw themselves as patriots. In high school sports they had earned recognition as heroes. Kat knew that if she looked hard enough, she could find the personal reasons they defined themselves as they did – authoritarian fathers in at least some cases, she suspected. Life is a search for balance, and the four men had sought it by acting outside the law. Kat believed they all thought they were doing a good thing.

Elliott Langston and Patricia Gibbs had thought they were doing good things, as well. They had been shaped by the circumstances of their upbringing, and their needs had put them on a collision course with these men.

Kat looked out at the harbor – at a view that went on for miles across the water. Duncan was examining a wooden post, reading the mail, happy in his own world.

Kat's own unfulfilled need was for the love she never got from an alcoholic and abusive mother. She imagined the self-loathing her mother must have felt for that – the ultimate betrayal of a child. Kat had been cheated in the worst way, and it would have easily justified a life of bitterness and self-pity. She could never forgive her mother, but could have told her she understood, except that she couldn't even do that now because her mother was gone.

To survive, Kat had fled from her mother and lived as a feral creature in the Adirondack woods of New York, breaking into cabins and summer homes for food and shelter. It would be easy to throw her life away and blame her mother, but who would that hurt? Not her deceased mother. Not now.

Her mother had dealt with pain the only way she knew, by numbing herself with alcohol till she died.

Tears were streaming down Kat's face, and she buried her head in her hands. She hoped no one was watching – this was unbecoming of a law officer. She tried never to show this vulnerable part of herself to Guy or Shane, but they knew.

It was just luck she had broken into a house on Pursuit Lake a few years ago where Shane and his friends were staying. They had caught her and turned her life around. If not for that, where would she be now?

Her husband could also have chosen a life of self-pity for the injustices done to his native people, but instead had chosen the opposite. Natives had a poor image among many whites – lazy, unmotivated, alcoholic, living on government handouts. Most whites did not understand their culture. Against the odds, Guy had gone to the university, studied and become a marine biologist. A native biologist working with white colleagues had to be better, had to work harder and smarter, and he did. Kat and Guy both were beating the odds. They both had something to prove.

Kat thought about *Duncan*. Whatever unfair start he'd had in life, he was a survivor, a happy warrior. His irrepressible good nature was why she needed him in her life so much, a constant reminder to live in the present, in the moment, and be grateful for each good new thing that came her way.

Give a dog love and he'll give it right back to you

all day long. It's what Kat needed, and everyone else, too.

Kat sensed she was on the brink of arresting Marlene Meyers for the murder of both victims. It would be the final chapter in a political career marked by greed, anger and a shocking willingness to jettison democratic processes. All she needed was for Larry Ward to say the name – say that Marlene was The Boss who had given him the orders. Kat would have Tulare police make the arrest on an out-of-state warrant. Given Marlene's fiery rhetoric about taking back state government by force, Kat imagined they would be only too glad to expedite her return to Island County.

Ward and his lawyer filed into the interrogation room, flanked by Shane Lindstrom and Kat. Everyone took a seat at the table. Shane and Kat looked at the lawyer.
"We'd like to talk about a plea deal," the lawyer began.
"I'm afraid you waited a little too long, unless you're prepared to tell us about The Boss," Kat replied.

Kat and Shane sat in their cruiser in front of Gibbs's real estate office and watched for the white Escalade. After twenty minutes, at nine a.m., Kat spotted the vehicle in her rear-view mirror.
"There he is," she said. "He's coming up on us now."
Gibbs drove past them, stopped in the street, and backed up to parallel park. The two officers got out of their vehicle and approached him on both sides of his car. Gibbs shut off the engine and powered down the window.
"This is a surprise," he said to Kat.
"Mr. Gibbs," she responded, "Step out of the car,

please. I'm arresting you for the murders of Elliott Langston and Patricia Gibbs."

He turned white.

"*What?*" he exclaimed. "Patty? My own sister? You've got to be kidding. I don't understand. I never murdered anyone. You're making a huge mistake here."

"Step out of the vehicle, please," Kat repeated. "Turn around and place your hands on the roof," Kat continued. "You have the right to remain silent ..."

She patted him down.

"Hands behind your back, please."

He did as instructed and Kat snapped handcuffs on his wrists.

*

Walter Gibbs shuffled into the interrogation room with his lawyer behind him. Gibbs's face was drawn. The lawyer was a prominent criminal defense specialist from Mount Vernon. It struck Kat that this case was providing full employment for the legal profession, with all the plea deals that were being negotiated. Delaney and Ward already had hired the two best on the island.

Kat switched on the video recorder and everyone identified themselves for the tape.

"Before we begin," Gibbs said, "would you please explain some things to me? Was my sister, Patty, identified as one of the victims? And what is the evidence suggesting I had anything to do with those murders?"

"Your sister was positively identified by DNA," Kat replied. "And we have a witness who identifies you as The Boss, the individual who ordered and paid for the murder of Elliott Langston. One of the shooters is in custody and cooperating. The other is deceased."

"How did my sister get involved?" he asked,

shaking his head. "She lived in California at the time of her disappearance."

"Your sister traveled to Whidbey Island, arriving the day of the murders, and was with Elliott Langston when he was shot. Her involvement appears to have been coincidental. She was a witness who had to be eliminated."

"I don't understand," he said. "What was she doing here?"

"Apparently, trying to stop you from doing what you were doing," Kat said.

Gibbs let out a wail and buried his head in his hands. His whole body, the large mound of flesh, was shaking.

"I knew ..." he blubbered, "she ... felt," he took a breath, "felt strongly ... about her Buddhist principles." He was searching for words. "I had no idea ... we hadn't talked for a year. Why didn't she say something?"

"I think we'd better recess this session," Gibbs's lawyer said, placing his hand on Gibbs's forearm. "My client needs some time to digest what he has just heard."

"Do you want to come back to this tomorrow, Mr. Gibbs?" Kat asked.

"No. Yes. This doesn't make any sense."

"We'll step out and let you confer with your lawyer," Kat said. "We'll continue this interview tomorrow." She switched off the recorder, and she and Shane left the room.

As she and Shane closed the door behind them, Kat remarked, "Well, that answers one thing."

"What's that?"

"He didn't know about Patty."

"What in the hell is going on?" Marlene Meyers asked. "I can't reach anyone who will tell me."

It was early morning and she was sitting alone at

her desk in the Tulare office park, amid boxes of campaign literature, flags, placards and buttons. Meyers signs were stacked against the walls of the room, ready for her staff to distribute in a few hours.

At this early hour Meyers was holding her cell phone to her ear. Later this morning, hundreds of her supporters would stage a march down Visalia's Mooney Boulevard as a show of strength in her campaign for the legislature, but right now she could not stop thinking about what was happening back on the island.

The front page of the *Times-Delta*, on the desk in front of her, carried a large article and photograph of Patricia Gibbs, a local woman who disappeared in 2008, whose skeletal remains had been found underneath an Oak Harbor street. It was sensational news.

"Larry Ward has been arrested," said the voice in Marlene's ear, a long-time night jailer in Coupeville. They've charged him with two murders and he's right here in the lockup, pending bail."

"What about Walter?"

"He's here, too."

"He was arrested?"

"That's right."

This meant Ward must have fingered Gibbs, but what had Gibbs said? All bets were off, now that Gibbs had just learned his own sister was one of the victims.

Gibbs paced in his cell – he couldn't sleep. He knew Larry Ward was just down the line a few cells, but had no desire to talk to him. During the night, things had gotten noisy when deputies brought in an aggressive, highly agitated twenty-something who had threatened his girlfriend with a knife. The kid was screaming and hollering, "I'll kill that bitch."

This was a side of life he'd never seen in his many years as a developer and respected member of Oak

Harbor's business community, and a deacon in his church. The kid was snoring now and things had quieted down.

Every so often, the night jailer made the rounds to check on them. "Everything okay?" he asked. "You should get some sleep."

"Can't sleep," Gibbs said.

"That happens. It'll get easier."

Gibbs guessed the jailer's job was partly to watch for suicide risks. *Was he depressed? Could he be thinking about suicide?* The quiet of the night no doubt was when the doubts crept closer for many inmates, if they were going to.

Gibbs had been allowed one ten-minute phone call to Judy, his wife. It hadn't gone well. "What is going on?" she asked. "What have you done? Do I even know you anymore?"

"It's a mistake," Gibbs said. "We'll get it straightened out and I'll be home soon. Do me a favor, okay?" he asked. "Get someone to drive you down to the office and retrieve the Escalade, and bring it home."

"Are you a murderer?" Judy blurted. "What kind of man murders his own sister? I'm trying to understand that." Gibbs had no answer.

Today was Sunday and Judy would be in church in a few hours. Friends would put their arms around her and say, "Oh Judy, I heard the news. I'm so sorry," not wanting to spell out exactly what they'd heard. For Judy it would be supremely embarrassing, the worst day of her life, accepting their sympathy while still unable to understand what had happened.

Walter could imagine what was going through her mind. She would already realize that if he was guilty, this was the end of their real estate business, their livelihood, their home. It seemed impossible they could go on being married. Walter felt the weight of what he had done to Judy, the ultimate betrayal.

But greater than that was the shame he felt over what he had done to Patty. Without knowing it, he had been complicit in the murder the one person he loved more than anyone else in the world. He and Patty had grown up with different ideas, different expectations of what they wanted from life, but always secure in each other's love. They had wanted the best for each other. Apparently, she had felt so strongly about her spiritual search that she had tried to steer Walter away from the course he was on. Patty had never known wealth – just peace. Walter had never known peace, and now never would.

Larry Ward laid on his cot in his orange jump suit, eyes open, staring at the ceiling. He was aware of the night jailer passing by, studying him. This was not where he'd expected to be in his seventies. He'd expected to be at Marlene's side, sharing the triumph of her rise to power. The prospect of living ten or fifteen more years behind bars, in a penitentiary, was beyond imagination. He did not think he could endure it.

Ward's lawyer was trying to negotiate a plea deal, but Ward was feeling expendable for the first time in his life. It had finally caught up with him. He had been in Marlene's thrall since high school. She was now a thousand miles away and he was mired in an old mess that was just getting worse and worse.

Two cells down from Gibbs, Dennis Delaney was thinking about the view from his tractor and the freshly mown field he had left for Manuel. The morning light, the aroma of grass and diesel, and the comforting rattle of the mower were memories he might never know again. The hardest thing would be not seeing Alicia.

In his mind he was going over his prospects. He knew that Larry Ward, whom he had identified as "The

Boss," had been arrested and was now behind bars just down the cellblock from him. He didn't have much feeling of loyalty to Larry, who had always struck him as arrogant, and wondered if Ward had had something to do with Ryan Ashford's death. The bond the wrestlers had shared a lifetime ago had long since unraveled.

Times change, and the political truths that had seemed so obvious to Delaney decades ago no longer applied. The world was a different place and he was a different man. The whole murder-for-hire plot had been a mistake. He hoped that by giving up Ward's name, and what had happened to Christy Morris, he had done enough to gain clemency that would spare him hard prison time for murder.

For Alicia, memories of a past life came flooding back – her last look at home. She was sitting in a twin-engine Cessna 310, its engines roaring as the pilot advanced the throttles and held the brakes. The jungle clearing amplified everything. At last he released the brakes and the plane accelerated down the grassy strip, slowly at first, its wings rocking as it bounced over bumps.

As it gained speed, it skipped once or twice, briefly airborne and then touching back to Earth again. Alicia couldn't take her eyes off the trees at the far end of the clearing. She was terrified. At last, the pilot pulled back on the yoke and the plane jumped into the air, blue sky filling the windshield, clearing the trees by what seemed like only feet.

Dennis and his men would now melt into the jungle, gone from her life. If she reached the United States, she would have to become someone new.

Alicia felt the right wing dip sharply. She was looking at the ground as the aircraft banked north, still just above the jungle canopy. At one point she glimpsed several men pointing rifles at the sky, but they were past them in an instant. The pilot seemed unconcerned. "We don't give them time to react," he said. "Once we reach the coast, we'll stay low and out of radar range. From there on, I don't expect much trouble."

Fifteen years later, Alicia looked out at a half-mown field on their Oregon ranch – as far as Dennis had gotten on that last day. Time had stopped for her. The flight to Whidbey Island and back had been her first in a small plane since Dennis led her to the jungle airstrip and put her on the CIA aircraft to Miami. He had given her a briefcase and a revolver, and a cover story in case anyone asked. She was a courier with top-secret materials.

He had taken a risk for her and she would stand by him now and carry on the work of the farm with Manuel's help. It would be harder now. Their story, the shadowy lives they had left behind in the jungle decades ago, would come out. Their relationships in the farming community were gone. The ag association would immediately replace her husband as president and try to put the scandal behind them. The bank would be unlikely to extend any more financing for equipment or crops. Life as they knew it would never be the same, even if Dennis somehow gained release.

Mercury vapor lamps illuminated the buildings of the Tulare office park in a cold blue light. It was still an hour before the first pale hint of dawn would backlight the sky. Tulare police waited in the shadows, their vehicles tucked out of sight behind surrounding buildings. Marlene Meyers was an early riser, and given her ability to mobilize a crowd, the plan was to make the arrest quietly, before others arrived to witness it.

The department had cancelled all officer leave and called in extra patrols from other departments in case the arrest triggered violent protests. Marlene's BMW came down the drive and rolled to a stop right in front of the door. Officers approached the car from both sides, flashed their ID, and asked her to get out.

She unrolled the driver's window. "What is this about, officer?" she asked in her breathless whisper.

"You are a person of interest in the murder of Elliott Langston and Patricia Gibbs," the officer replied. "We need you to come down to the station and answer a few questions."

"You're out of your minds," Marlene protested in a much louder, more commanding tone. "Do you know who I am? Whatever this is about, you're making a big mistake."

"We'd like you to come with us," the arresting officer stated. "You can call your lawyer and we'll go from there."

In the sheriff's interrogation room in Coupeville, Kat and Shane sat across from Larry Ward and his lawyer.

"There is no boss, is there?" Kat asked. "The Boss is you."

"I told you, The Boss is Walter Gibbs," Ward protested. "It was his real estate development and he had everything to lose if it fell through."

"I don't believe you," Kat said. "Gibbs admits he knew there was talk about murdering Elliott Langston and blames himself for failing to speak up and stop it. He thought Marlene Meyers was behind it, and if she was, a person with her power could ruin him. But she wasn't, was she?" Kat asked. "It was just you, trying to impress her. And now you're trying to shift the blame to Walter Gibbs in hopes of reducing your own culpability and getting a lighter sentence in a plea deal."

"Do you have any evidence to corroborate that?" Ward's lawyer asked.

"We have the testimony of Marvin Trammel and Dennis Delaney that you directed their actions. We have Walter Gibbs's testimony that he knew of your plan. We have Marlene Meyers's testimony that, at no time, did she ask anyone to murder anybody."

Ward shook his head.

"That leaves you, Mr. Ward. All alone. You're going to prison for the rest of your life."

"I never killed anyone," Ward said – not Elliott Langston, not Patricia Gibbs, not Ryan Ashford and not Christy Morris."

Kat and Shane sat at their desks and looked at each other. Shane took a sip of his coffee. Kat twirled a lock of her hair.

"Do you think Larry Ward was the mastermind all along?" Shane asked.

"Oh no. Not at all. It's just a question of whether he's ready to talk. He's facing life. His girlfriend is about to get elected to the California state senate. He has taken the fall for her and doesn't have anything to show for a lifetime of keeping secrets."

Kat's phone rang. "This is the jailer," the caller said. "Larry Ward would like to talk with you."

When Kat and Shane arrived at the jail, the guard showed them to Larry Ward's cell. He was sitting on the edge of his bunk, looking at the floor. It was the first time Kat had seen him downcast. Always before, he had projected a cocky self-confidence.

"I'd like to give you a full accounting," he said.

"Please do."

"It was Marlene who ordered the murder of Elliott Langston. He was blocking approval of the Gibbs Addition, which tied up hundreds of thousands of dollars of her investment."

"What I don't understand," Kat said, "is where she got the power to make the four of you carry out her orders."

"We did a terrible thing in high school and Marlene knew about it. We were drinking and ran down Christy Morris with Ryan's automobile and covered it up. Marlene held that over us and we knew she could tell the police if we didn't go along with her. We all wanted military careers, and doubted that any branch would have us if they knew."

"I already knew," Kat said.

Larry looked up. "You did?"

"Dennis Delaney told me. It was weighing on his conscience."

"What they probably didn't know was that I was the one who told Marlene about Christy. I wanted to help Marlene. A couple of the others – Dennis and Marvin – were very troubled about killing Elliott and the woman who was with him. Marvin was sick about his role in transporting the bodies to the hole. I had to do something to keep the group together."

"So you'll testify against her?"

"Yes," Larry said, his voice breaking.

"Roger will be proud of you," Shane said. "This was his hardest case and he always felt bad that it ended with nothing – not even a body."

"I hope Roger feels good about it," Kat said. "Finding the bodies was just luck. I filled in Roger last night on how things turned out. I wanted to do that before the newspapers and TV stations got ahold of it. But I worry that we may not yet have the full story."

"The sheriff is planning a press conference for ten o'clock this morning," Shane said. "He's pretty happy to have some arrests in such an old case."

"Ward was loyal to Marlene for the longest time. He never turned on her," Shane said.

"She never turned on him, either. "Do you think she loved him?"

"I don't know. Did she ever love anyone except herself? I can't find any evidence of it. She used him, and I think he finally figured that out. Ward was a zealot and was the perfect lieutenant for her. He remained a lifelong bachelor. Whether she actually loved him, we may never know, and he'll have lots of time to think about that now."

Kat was looking around, her gaze focused out the window at the blue sky and at her cruiser, sitting under a shade tree in the parking lot. "Right now, I think I could use a little fresh air."

"Really?" Shane asked. "Where are you headed?"

"Double Bluff Beach. I have a walking date."

Shane looked out the window at Kat's cruiser. The windows were all rolled down and a polka-dot nose was facing their way.

The Complete Mystery Series
Available from Whidbey Island bookstores and online from Amazon.com in paperback and Kindle versions.

Final Deception: *A Whidbey Island Mystery*

In the blackness, Bella Morelli pitched face forward in an ungainly dive, wind roaring in her ears. The four seconds took forever and she had two last thoughts – surprise and dread. She hit the water all wrong like a breaching whale, lungs first, a horrible impact, and that was the last she felt.

Deception Pass Bridge connects Washington's Fidalgo and Whidbey islands across a deep chasm. It is 180 feet from the bridge deck to the water, depending on tide. From there it's 130 more in icy darkness to the bottom.

A young person in peak condition, hitting the water feet first in perfect form, can survive if they miss the rocks and regain the surface before drowning or hypothermia. A 67-year-old cannot. Whirlpools and eddies reach out to clutch and pull them down.

Decades ago, Brad had almost cracked the mystery of Bella. She had taken a road trip with him, taken a risk. Brad registered them in a Tennessee motel as Mr. and Mrs. Brad Haraldsen.

They hadn't discussed the sleeping arrangement – it just happened. They were two unmarried 25-year-olds traveling in the South in 1972. Gatlinburg was a honeymoon destination and the couple's eyes glistened with new love. Even in civilian attire, Brad carried himself with military bearing. That and his clean-cut, neatly trimmed hair were assets in the South where patriotism ran high.

As it was, the clerk didn't question their marital status – gave them a room by the pool in the nearly vacant auto court.

A heavy sky threatened afternoon lightning. Brad and Bella swam anyway and washed the miles from the road. Then, five years into their friendship, they made love for the first time as comfortably as if it were every day.

The lovemaking was slow and satisfying, their private secret as the storm rumbled through the lush hills beyond the thick curtains. Afterwards, they lay in each other's arms. Bella smiled and Brad felt her caution about him wash away.

A lifetime later, sitting on his mountain in Stanley, Idaho, Brad still teared up at the memory, as vivid now as it had ever been. That time, that place to which they had never returned, was the happiest of his life. Brad's eyes stung and he closed them to see it all again. He remembered every detail of that motel, that room, the long journey that led there.

Final Passage: *Mystery on the Alaska Ferry*

The Matanuska inches ahead between flashing navigation buoys in Wrangell Narrows, changing course at each marker to stay within this twisting channel. Evening is falling and a campfire burns brightly on shore a hundred yards away. Sweet smoke from the fire drifts over the ship and takes Brad back to times he and Irene spent in the mountains of Idaho with their friends of a lifetime, Stu and Amy, both now gone. It's a bittersweet memory.

Brad imagines a family around that campfire, roasting weenies and marshmallows, or maybe good friends talking about their day. Smoke drifts toward the ferry from woodstoves in cozy cabins so close they could shout to the owners. A dog barks. A couple standing on their deck wave to the ship and Brad waves back.

Waltersburg is a storybook scene on this quiet night. Irene is glad she made the effort to stay up. The lights of the town and its many boats must hold a thousand secrets of ordinary people and their Alaska-size dreams on the edge of the civilized world.

Moonlight bathes the snowfields of nearby peaks. This is the prettiest place she has seen on this trip, a pocket of humanity in the heart of wilderness, surrounded by water, mountains, glaciers and forest. She has this moment to herself, the other passengers having retired to their cabins for the evening. She lingers a while, then starts a leisurely circuit around the deck, taking in the view and the aromas of creosoted pilings, fish canneries, fir trees . . .

The impact from behind knocks the wind from Irene's lungs and sends her reeling forward, fighting for balance. She grabs wildly for the rail with her right arm and barely catches it, staying half on her feet, unable to breathe. Her heart pounds and her legs fold. She wraps her body over the rail and gasps in shock, staring down at the white bubbles where the bow slices through the blackness. Half a minute passes with no air. She's in full panic.

Then, ever so slowly, her diaphragm responds and her lungs draw air. She straightens up and wonders what happened. She is alone on the deck – no passengers, no crew. The ship already is in open water, accelerating toward Juneau.

Final Escape: *Mystery in the Idaho Sawtooths*

On the porch after dinner, Brad breaks out two Mt. Borah Brown Ales for Shane and himself while Elizabeth and Irene clink glasses of wine. Brad notices Elizabeth looks especially beautiful in the soft light of the early evening, her long red hair catching the sun. Did she fix herself up a little extra? He catches Shane's eyes lingering on her.

In the distance, the soulful melody of a harmonica floats their way on the breeze.

"That's Bolivar," Brad says, "introducing Freddie to the harmonica. He's not bad, don't you think?"

Brad explains to Shane that the ale comes from a small craft brewery in Salmon, several hours north. "I think it's a delicious beer and it brings back memories of the time I climbed Mt. Borah in the Air Force."

"You were 20-something?" Shane asks.

"Yeah. About that."

"Reliving past glories," Shane laughs.

"Exactly."

Irene interjects. "He has a rich fantasy life."

Brad stares at her with a knowing smile. "I happen to like my fantasies," and then back at Shane. "Seriously, Shane, while Freddie is with Bolivar and we have a few minutes, I wanted to ask your advice about a problem Elizabeth is having."

Shane leans forward and listens while Brad outlines the situation. When he finishes, Shane leans back and turns to Elizabeth, "Is it the same guy?"

"I don't think so."

"Because of the black hair? The pony tail?"

"Mainly that."

"I think it might be him," he says. "Otherwise, it's an awfully big coincidence. It wouldn't be a hard disguise."

Brad adds, "There's something else. I didn't mention this to Elizabeth earlier, but we've started getting some harassing phone messages and hang-ups here at the ranch."

Final Justice: *Mystery on Whidbey Island*

At the clearing's edge, where the tall grass and brush gives way to trees, a man begins to dig. It's a remote spot some distance from an isolated building at the end of a private, forest lane nobody uses. Sweat runs down the man's forehead from his bald head and stings his eyes. From his back pocket he extracts a red bandanna and ties it across his forehead.

The man digs three large sword ferns with generous root balls and sets them aside on a tarp with the rest of the dirt from the hole.

A feeling grows inside him that he's not alone. Heart pounding, he stops, straightens up and looks around for something that does not belong. He scans the trees and shadows, and suddenly registers two large, yellow eyes and sharp-pointed ears staring right at him. It's a Great-horned Owl thirty feet away in a fir tree, backlit in the shadows. The owl follows every move; its eyes unnerve him seeming to know too much.

The two beings study each other, neither breaking his gaze. Then finally, the man turns his back and returns to his work. With a pick he breaks loose a little of the coble and scoops it out of the hole with his shovel, then goes back to the pick. He feels those eyes watching the back of his head.

*

At Jerry's cabin near Possession Point, Judy studies the paperclip on the floor, just beyond reach of her foot. She is handcuffed by one wrist to the bed. Because of the handcuffs, she can't turn her body around very comfortably to face the wall, but the wall is her only hope at this point.

With pain shooting up her arm to the shoulder joint, she twists her body till one foot reaches the wall. She pushes against it and the bed moves an inch. She does it again, more painfully, and the bed moves some more. Each push is harder and more excruciating than the one before, but each moves the bed precious inches toward the paperclip.

Final Pursuit: *Mystery in the Adirondacks*

Something brushed Shane Lindstrom's shoulder as he slept. His wife, Elizabeth, lay beside him and he was pretty sure she'd touched him on purpose – lightly, so as not to startle him. The bed was deliciously warm and he willed himself not to move. He didn't want to awaken. When she did it a second time, it was sharp. "Somebody's in the house!" she whispered urgently.

"Huh? He mumbled, turning to face her. "Didn't you hear it? A window sliding open downstairs."

"Are you sure? Not just the breeze?"

"There's no breeze."

Shane glanced at the café curtains in the bedroom window, dimly backlit by a quarter moon. They hung straight and still on this humid night. Beyond them lay Pursuit Lake and a handful of cabins linked by shoreline trails. How could anyone be prowling downstairs?

. . . The next sound was unmistakable – a metallic crash and muffled moan in the kitchen below them. The moan was human and Shane was wide awake now, too. He pictured someone lowering himself through the pantry window from the screened deck, probing for the floor with his dangling feet and kicking the galvanized pail Shane had left by the window in preparation to mop the floor . . . Shane folded back the sheet, swung his legs out of bed and stood. . .

Stepping into his pants in the darkness, he fastened his belt, then slid open the bedside drawer and felt for the reassuring bulk of his Glock. In the drawer beside it was a high-intensity tactical flashlight, which he slipped into his pocket. It could temporarily blind an intruder.

Final Impulse: *Mystery on Whidbey Island*

"Your wife," she began, "you are getting divorce?"

"Yes, we're in the process," George said. "It takes a while."

"She's gone how long?"

"Oh, for some time. I don't hear from her at all."

"You need to, what is the word, redecorate more manly," she said with a little laugh.

Nadya could still recite some of George's profile from memory. *Unattached male, professional, engineer, virile and youthful, seeks adventurous partner, thirtyish, for walks on the beach, cozy dinners, romantic getaways. Thinking marriage.*

It all sounded good and she liked the word "marriage," but everything hinged on that other word, "unattached."

Nadya continued her tour of the house.

"This door," she said. "Is for where?"

"The garage and workshop," George said. "I keep it locked.

"Let me show you the bedroom," George said, leading her in the opposite direction and down the hall.

Nadya noted the king bed looked like it had been

made up by a man, not too precisely. That was typical. Working as a maid in a hotel, Nadya had learned to make perfect hospital corners. She had also cleaned up after many guests who had behaved like animals and left their disgusting fluids on the sheets. That was the seamier side of her job.

She wondered what it would be like to make love to this man tonight in this bed, in this room. They hadn't discussed the sleeping arrangement in their letters and calls, but the long-distance flirting and sexual tension were high. Of course, it's easy over the phone for the mind to fill in some details that don't always conform to the real world.

Her girlfriend, Vanya, said she was a hopeless romantic. It was probably true. Nadya wanted a storybook love – maybe a little too much.

Final Descent: *A Whidbey Island Mystery*

Thanksgiving Eve, 1971. Swinging beneath the parachute canopy, Cooper could see a handful of lights in the distance – outlying houses and a small community. Families were eating dinner in those cozy houses, watching TV, relaxing by a warm fire on the evening before the big meal.

He struggled to recognize the town, to orient himself, but couldn't.

Gusty winds were carrying him rapidly cross-country. Patches of this forest had been logged, and the stumps and debris in those clear cuts scared him more than the forest. In the darkness below there would be trees. They were the better of two bad options . . .

Something brushed his legs – the soft, bent to of a hemlock. He clutched his chest and the pack full of money. Wham, wham, wham, he felt as his body raked the side branches, snapping brittle stubs from the trunk as he fell. The pack protected his midsection but pain shot through his shoulder and ribs. A branch scraped his face. Then nothing.

Final Reunion: *Murder at Useless Bay*

"You can pull her up on the beach now, said Dr. Ralph Emerson, the county coroner. Shane and Kat put on plastic gloves and each took an arm. It was hard to do this in a respectful way. Handling the dead was a part of this job Kat found wrenching. She was a cop, not an undertaker.

The woman's head lolled back, and Kat knew Shane didn't want to drag it in the sand any more than she did. They lifted her higher.

When they had scooted the body several feet onto the shore, they lowered her arms to the sand and Shane searched her pockets. He turned the body slightly and reached around her collar, and patted the sides and butt of her pants. He also inspected her wrists and hands.

"Nothing but this gold necklace with a dog on it," he said to Kat, examining the piece of jewelry in his hand. "No cell phone, no I.D. Did any of these people find anything nearby – a purse or jacket?"

Final Remains: *Mystery at Ebey's Landing*

In the foamy surf at the toe of the bluff, something lavender and white caught Nadya Komaresch's eye. It was man-made, attracting the last rays of sunset, perhaps a colorful net float or athletic shoe carried on the tide.

With each advance of the frothy surf, the object scooted higher up the beach. Then, as the water receded, it ran part way back to the sea. It played in the waves, turning lengthwise, then broadside,

FINAL COVER-UP

tumbling upside down, rolling and stopping right side up. She'd take a closer look when she walked back on the beach in a few minutes.

*

When a human foot washes ashore at Ebey's Landing near Coupeville on Whidbey Island, Sheriff's Deputy Katarina Brown gets the call to investigate. Kat's inquiries take her deep into the lives of five missing women, and the circumstances that could have led them here.

DAN PEDERSEN

About the Author

Dan Pedersen grew up in Western Washington. He holds two journalism degrees from the University of Washington and worked as a reporter and editor for several newspapers in Idaho and Washington, including a large outdoor weekly. He also managed publications for a financial services corporation. He is the author of sixteen books, ten of which are mysteries.

He writes a weekly blog about nature and rural living, Dan's Blog, which may be found at www.pedersenwrites.blogspot.com.